Shepherd and the Lost Sheep

A Motherless Child

Craig Kanyemba

Shepherd and the lost sheep: A Motherless Child

Published by Apadana
Johannesburg, South Africa
kanyembacraig0@gmail.com

ISBN 978-0-620-78937-0

2 4 6 8 10 9 7 5 3

Layout and cover design by Boutique Books
Printed in South Africa by Digital Action

Dear God, my first letter to you

Thank you everyone for your support:
my family and all my friends,
I really appreciate all of you.

Craig Kanyemba

Thank you,

Tarrin

Jeremiah 50:6

My people have been lost sheep.
Their shepherds have led them astray
and turned them loose in the mountains.
They have lost their way
and can't remember how to get back
to the sheepfold.

Everyone has missed the point.
Africa had no wild sheep until recently.

Stop
Drug
Abuse
Be Free
Stop drinking Syrup

- I have never came across a drug that is as controversial as ***Nyaope***. It has allegedly come into widespread use, especially in impoverished settlements. This drug contains antiretroviral drugs and is smoked in the form of a joint, mixed with cannabis. Its effects last for two to four hours.

- ***Blood diamonds*** (also called conflict diamonds, war diamonds, hot diamonds or red diamonds) is a term used for a diamond mined in a war zone and sold to finance an insurgency, an invading army's war efforts, or a warlord's activities. The term is used to highlight the negative consequences of the diamond trade in certain areas, or to label an individual diamond as having come from such an area. Diamonds mined during the recent civil wars in Angola, Ivory Coast, Sierra Leone and other nations have been given the label.

Chapter One

01h00 Thursday

Rejected, disrespected and well reflected, he knew that there was no time to go back. Poverty had pushed him this far, and probably hell flames were burning for him. He held a yellowish powder in his left hand and a razor blade in his right. He crushed it together with mixtures of different antiretroviral drugs. He was a boy aged fourteen, hiding in a corner covered in darkness, smoking substances into his head.

Brainwashed by a fake life briefcase containing hype, fame (an empty bubble), money and girls, "*paper chasing*" remained the motto his heart loved most. No one is ever too young to be a dream chaser, but for many their dreams remain elusive – or delusive.

A FEW HOURS LATER, GUNFIRE sounded five blocks away, awakening everybody. It was a disturbing sound at that hour. What evil has been done again? It's 02h00 and the morning is still young. By 03h00 the hospital opened its emergency doors. The surgery ward had everyone awake and active. Bullets fired into the man's lungs had caused irrecoverable damage.

"He's got less than a five percent chance of survival. If we do not hurry, it's zero," Doctor Choo said before the operation began. The patient had lost a lot of blood at the point of injury. Everyone became alert and extra careful.

One of the nurses kept on screaming, "Tell me, who did this to you?" like the paramedics had failed to keep him awake for such questions. "Who did this to you?" she asked, broken-hearted. It was a situation that words could not express.

Everything was moving as fast as one would find in a restaurant kitchen when clients are pumping in to have a good time on a Sunday afternoon. The only words the wounded man, in his early forties, said were: "They should give them the education they need". He fought for this small speech, the words struggling to come out of his mouth one by one, making his last breath very important.

THE PHONE RANG THREE TIMES at a certain station. After ignoring it for a while, enjoying the sweet taste of his cigarette, an officer walked to it from a distance. Then he grabbed it and picked up the call. "Can you please state your emergency?" His words were sort of like these; there was no effort to say them correctly, and he shortened the daily routine.

Some woman was crying. There seemed to be a kind of pandemonium, a numbness of noise. The caller screamed at the top of her lungs, although it was more like crying. All she could say for the first thirty seconds on the phone was, "I think he's dead!" After a while, the officer realised that the call might be a serious one. When the penny had dropped, he kept on asking the crying lady many questions: Where was she? What had happened to her?

"Ma'am, can you calm down," he urged first, but she could not do that with her eyes on the victim.

"I think! Wait a minute," she was stammering on a very high note. "I think! Hold on! He is breathing," she called out on the phone, and she then said, "He looked too young to do such a horrible thing". This seemed to scare everything out of her.

A few minutes later, the police radio in police vehicles in the city notified a new report to the police officers: Shots were fired on the other side of the city. The nearest squad car was to go in with full body armour as it was a dangerous situation. They might run into the perpetrators; sometimes they ran into failed missions.

“WHERE IS THE CAR?” TINASHE whispered to the man who was standing in a corner with its dark covering his whole face. He knew exactly the spot and he could see him, even in the dark.

Foster did not answer. He had a question set aside already for Tinashe. “Are those the packages?” he asked.

“Yes,” Tinashe answered, and Foster said, “What are we waiting for then?” and they passed around the corner. The engine was still running. Foster went to the driver’s seat, taking over. Tinashe followed him, before he was left behind. What he had in his hands were what Foster had referred to as packages: a transient, shining trouble. They both got into the car.

SOME MOMENTS LATER, A MAN in his late twenties came to the scene. He was now standing near other officers. They were talking as he handed across a notebook with black covers. Some officers were holding recorders and smalls pads, asking questions that might start a trail of some sort, or add to the evidence. All the lights were off. “What has been stolen might make people disappear.”

In the previous two weeks a bank hit had delivered millions and the crime rate on a gangster continent had spiked. A lot of brown envelopes were moving around for private payments.

The trail of what had happened at this crime scene and the answers were not of any help, providing nothing meaningful to what they knew.

“TINASHE, YOU WILL GET YOUR share. You are a brave man. Such accidents occur very quickly to those who forget to donate to the charity.” Foster promised the young person a good portion. Sitting at the back, Tinashe held closely to two rounded bags with cheap designs. They were having their chat in a shiny red car that had tinted windows. Tinashe looked paranoid and nervous, and more scared than he would on a normal day in his life. He glanced outside at the rapidly moving images of city lights. He was mumbling a song he'd once heard and had repeated so many times: *Rear-view Mirror*.

An officer wearing a brownish suit jacket with black trousers, got out of a Ford. He was after a notebook from one of the officers who was taking down the information from eye witnesses. It was a notebook with the information from a screaming, crying lady in her sixties who had recently made a call to the police. Now she was calm and quiet. She had seen a lot in her days of living, but now she never stopped weeping. The notebook was handed to him, so that he could have a rapid look.

"Sir, this has turned into a murder crime scene. From all the information we were able to gather, it seems as if these were the activities of a minor, Sir!"

Detective Mduduzi, to whom this was addressed, saw more activity than Danny Glover and he laughed a lot whenever he was reminded of it by the other officers who worked with him. Reading and flipping pages over one by one he said, "It was done perfectly". He closed the notebook and gave it back. "Collect all the evidence and make a copy of it. I need it on my desk, as soon as possible." Yellow tape protected the entire crime scene.

The ambulance had taken the victim at 02h30 and possibly he was still conscious then. Detective Mduduzi went back to his car with his mind focused. He wanted to reach the hospital while the injured man was breathing and before anything serious, such as death, happened. Gunshot wounds are a threat to a human life; people should be careful about what kind of toys they keep. He shut the door and drove while playing morning jazz sounds on the car radio.

"Are we there yet?" Tinashe had asked the same question more than three or four times in every minute. When they approached, another car was outside the warehouse; it was along the road. Foster parked behind this vehicle. The warehouse gate had a rusty appearance and chemical spray paint designs. When Foster got out of his car to open the warehouse, he found it unlocked and assumed the Grand Cherokee's owner was inside the warehouse. The lights were all off and Tinashe felt panic, although Foster remained calm. This was the third man of the trinity.

Tinashe kept on looking at Foster's movements. It seemed the boy was not fully aware of the whole plan. Wearing a faded black leather coat, the other man's face was only to be reviewed as he walked closer to the lights that Foster had switched on. Foster introduced Tinashe to George.

"You are bolt Hussein, huh? Very fast. Already here."

"Yeah, yeah," George answered.

"Do you have the bags with you?" George asked, as he switched on all the lights. Tinashe was meant to get the bags but, not yet fully introduced to George, he had started disliking the man; he felt like he was unimportant. They took the bags from the car's back seat where Tinashe had left them. They passed them around between themselves, leaving Tinashe out. "Splendid achievement."

They had both opened the zips a quarter way, to check that they had not been played for fools. They both looked satisfied. "Evidence needs to be disposed of. Do you have a place now to dispose of it?" George murmured. Foster heard it quietly and understood it. It seemed the trouble was about to begin; you could see it just by looking in his eyes and his lips moving with prayers.

Tinashe's patience was running out. He was not involved and words or ideas of a done deal job were kept for future reference. Still, he had his eyes wide open so as not to miss any moment. He was not going to fall asleep until he had his share. This seemed like it might be a game for one player and that the cards were arranged in order and group sequence. Tinashe did not appreciate working like this.

THE FORD REACHED ITS POINT of destination and parked next to an ambulance that was off duty. Mduduzi's eyes could not help but to look for something that might feed his desperation for answers. A receptionist was writing down some information from a caller. Coming from the garage that was facing the hospital door from the opposite parking area, he stood there until she was done and asked her about the incident. "Can I please have the information about an individual who was brought in about fifteen minutes ago with gun wounds."

He's a police detective, she noticed, when he flashed his ID at her. "Down right," she said. "There are lifts. Let one take you to the second floor. You walk into the last room of the floor. And note that disturbance is prohibited." She added that rules apply to everyone; even the doctors take them seriously, especially when they are trying to save a life in such moments.

He pulled away his dark shades from his eyes. The darker the berry, the sweeter the juice, the female receptionist thought, wondering why he wore shades during such hours. The passage had very bright white lights as he walked down it. Nurses were already removing bloodstains from around the room. It spelled bad news for the detective and right away a nurse walked to him.

"You are a detective right?" she asked him and he nodded his head. "We could not get anything out of him to find his shooter while he was still breathing." She handed him a piece of paper on which was written: *They should give them the education they need*. These words related to something familiar. "That is all and thank you," she said. His interest in the story was aroused. She added, "We are moving the body to the mortuary, for your further investigation. You know the procedure." She walked away from him as his eyes were lost in the text on the paper.

He took the sealed plastic pack with bullet fragments out of a large envelope.

"Ma'am, can you please stay calm and describe what you saw and heard." The officer at the scene was asking all sorts of questions just to keep the action going. The woman told him a lot that went beyond the officer's expectation.

"Two security guards showed up here. I saw them after my morning prayers. Their visits are meant for the services of a casino close by – to collect or deliver money and I don't know exactly their other purposes," she explained. "One of them was suddenly shot while stepping out of the vehicle and nobody could see the shooter. Who it was or where he was coming from. Everything was just covered by darkness." She pointed out that, because of her old age, she hardly saw it clearly from a bedroom window. "I did not see who it was from that distance," she said.

The other security officer, who had fled at the shooting, was now busy explaining his whereabouts: why he had fled the scene like he was somehow involved, when all these things had occurred. All he could say was, "I should have saved him in time," but blaming and regretting cannot help. The damage had already been done. He kept on repeating the same words and he accepted that he had panicked.

"Let us use the river road; it might be safer for all of us." George got into his Grand Cherokee, and Foster got into his car. Foster was used to the M1 roads, but he suggested another one to George. They left with relief that at least the hard part of the job was over. Foster drover his red car back into the warehouse to store it there. They were all safe now. Tinashe had a happy smile on him, kissing poverty and a hungry stomach goodbye. The paranoia and jitteriness had faded away, and his heart was back at its normal pumping level. He just lay back and enjoyed the ride.

At around 06h00, the evidence was on the table with all the gathered up information necessary to tackle up the case. Detective Mduduzi was already walking into his office, ready to work, holding his brown cappuccino takeaway cup. He called the officer who had prepared the documents. “Thank you, warrant officer.” He looked at the files on the table while talking on the phone. He walked towards his window to open the curtains and increase the brightness in the office. Once he was done with it, he dropped the call quickly. He started working by putting everything from the evidence that was at his disposal together.

GEORGE TREATED TINASHE AS IF he were menial; the errand was over.

After they had driven a few kilometres from the warehouse, they pulled their car alongside the road and close to the riverbank. Two of them got out of the car and walked towards the river. Foster got out last, and went around to the boot to pull out a rifle with a black coat covering it. Tinashe was thinking that they were now separating ways, when he saw Foster approaching with a gun in his hand. He assumed that this was evidence that had to be destroyed. Nobody was smiling and that scared him a lot.

Even though he was high, he felt the loneliness of it all. He thought it was time for him to be paid for his work but the two men had different intentions for him. He had not imagined himself as the evidence that needed to be disposed of, wiped from the face of the earth.

George turned back, leaving Tinashe behind although he told him to walk on. “Kill him,” he whispered to Foster. “It is time”.

Tinashe stood at gunpoint: after all, Foster had promised him heaven on earth. Tinashe stepped back into the water as Foster approached him, all these things in his eyes. Even the thought of praying did not come to him. Even thoughts that God could save him did not occur.

Tinashe right away decided to take his chance before it was too late. Foster did not intend to actually put him down, but their mutual “friend” had no use for both of them alive. At some point eliminating them both was best for George. Tinashe turned back when Foster fired the first shot and missed him. He was already in the water; he had jumped in to find his life in there. Foster kept on shooting, not even in his direction, just to give a sense to George that he'd done what was necessary. After five shots, he threw the gun into the water.

As the detective was looking at the bullets, he recognised them straight away from a case six years ago. He'd once worked with a security company that had a connection with the army team. He murmured, "*What is the connection between all this,*" to himself. After spending more than two hours sitting at his desk thinking about it, he thought, "*There might be a probability of it; we almost solved it*".

Water was all-over his face. Breathing became harder and he pulled up his head with his eyes checking out. The water pressure pushed his body further and further away from the bank. Eventually, he managed to swim out of the water and sat on the riverbank. For that moment he felt the sweet, fresh breath of life within him. He took his time enjoying the sun rays that had enough heat in them to warm him up. His clothes were drying. Tinashe's shirt was torn on the side, and so were his trousers.

He placed both his hands on top of his head, holding his hair. He was still petrified by his thoughts. "*I was almost dead!*" Such thoughts tormented him and strengthened him for greater challenges to come. His heart was more angry than scared. He was no longer frightened; the fear in him had disappeared. Minutes later he stood up with a smile on his face and said aloud, "I am still healthy and alive, like I was yesterday". He also screamed out of a happy feeling. "I am not dead yet!"

The two crooks he had met had taught him a lesson of life. He'd needed one and, as they say, experience is the best teacher. "I want my share," he decided. He had had a chance of changing his life with the portion he was owed, so he followed the way that the vehicles had taken. It was up to him to find out where they had gone.

Detective Mduduzi picked up his ringing phone. "Hello, how have you been?" Joey asked over the phone. The detective thought, "W*hy am I not surprised*?" The conversation continued and the Colonel walked in. As the telephone call was important, Mduduzi started pointing fingers all over the information, moving them back and forth. He beckoned to the Police Colonel to look at the information and to find something to do while he was busy with the caller.

The Colonel's eyes looked at an old story, one he had already forgotten about. When Detective Mduduzi was off the phone, he raised many questions. "Southern empire arms dealerships again? They are back here?" Colonel said. "I thought they took care of it."

Detective Mduduzi replied, "Liars and crooks. I just got off the phone with Joey. He might be of help. Joey plants an evil seed and then lets it grow into the tallest tree in the middle of a garden."

Foster said to George, "It is done".

The car was moving fast and smaller cars opened the way to them, avoiding unnecessary accidents. George then said, "We'll just stop off at the heart and soul of the next town."

Foster wondered why George had wanted the boy done. He'd shown bravery all the way. Later, he remembered that George had a killer hand gene: he destroyed whatever stood in his path. Foster kept his mouth shut to avoid unnecessary troubles.

"Stupid things we do can get us in trouble," George said to Foster attentively. George added, "I was going to let the boy go, but I was afraid he was not going to keep his mouth to himself, after getting a little of that money".

Foster replied, "Yeah! I get you." He was not satisfied by how George was justifying his ruthless behaviour. Foster had brought Tinashe into the job. He'd mentioned his name in the first place for the third man in the robbery. After they had the money, nobody else was more important than they were. The conversation was already hectic between them and they were only waiting to reach the final destination.

Foster lost interest in chatting, although the money kept him waiting. The fact remained that it was blood money and until it reached the final destination, a lot of blood was going to be spilled. Someone could end up doing all the blood-shedding in the name of greed. Cars, women and all things luxurious were going to be the benefit of what they had retrieved from the private security guards, but one of the guards was already a victim. The bags sat on the seat, while a hand on the steering wheel and the other one on the gear stick accelerated the car to its limits.

HIS EYES WERE STILL LOOKING at the pieces of the six bullet fragments, but while staring at them his mind had travelled so far away that he could not follow it. He placed the small plastic pack into his drawer and pulled out his own notes about the crime observation. There were voice records from witnesses and he had every written note. He knew something was off from the fact that it was done by a young man. Going through the files one by one, his eyes widened as he looked at the picture of the victim. He had been shot by a skilled player. Mduduzi noticed the relationship between the current case and a case that was old and unsolved, and his curiosity grew like that of a fourteen year old. The kid had played a small part in the robbery; he did not fail to recognize that. That made his face brighter than before. *Incoming call.* He let it go straight to the message service. Whoever was on the phone was not as important at that moment as what he had figured out.

The phone rang again. He actually jumped to it, after a feeling a shock. Joey was on the phone. Mduduzi had worked with Joey Morish on a previous, although unsolved, case. “I will be there by eleven o’clock. Nothing has come, but maybe I will receive it when I get there and am ready at work. I look forward to meeting you again, friend."

Life of Tinashe

Rose had grown up with her mother in a very large ghetto. The story about her father stopped making sense when she reached her thirteenth birthday – a father whose story sounded like it had a rise and a sudden fall. She grew up broke and hungry all the time. Her mother had other babies and so she could not raise her properly, although she tried her best. The youngest of six, Rose was only a shadow in a big house.

Growing up, she was raped by her big brother a couple of times. When she reached seventeen, her games were out of control. At times she would go to school, but most of the time she diverted to her boyfriend's house, learning how to smoke and drink. She met a man way older than her. He spoiled her with every token, to the point that she lost focus. She made it to her eighteenth birthday pregnant. She fell out of love with the man, who had promised her heaven on earth. He learned that she was pregnant, and it only remained an untold story of her lifetime. She did think of a happily ever after, but knew it could not last to that point. He went solo, vanishing into thin air after the news had reached his ears. She was forced to find a job in order to support her child.

She gave birth to a son. One of her friends had thrown her baby away and she also thought of doing the same, but she was scared.

She was still young and many still wanted her. The money she got from her work was not even half of what she earned from different people who paid for her attention, and prostitution started. Five years later, raising Tinashe, she had only a three-day headache but it left her in a coffin.

Tinashe – Tinashe means *God is with us* – survived his grandmother's house which was more like a children's home; with his many other relatives, it was a church. The only language he understood was that of the streets. He grew into a teenager. They would beg for food when they were totally broke, which was all the time. Grandmother started getting ill from time to time. Him being her favourite, he was always beside her, until they lost her.

He became habituated to begging. It was only the beginning of it as jewellery, shoes and clothes were all under their ambitions. He had very high ambitions. Selling someone's drugs gave them enough for the night. Blankets were hidden in drains during the day and every night they would pick them up to make a bed. There were so many peers there was no need for pressure; they were all pushed to it by the way they were living. Shoplifting became one of the jobs for the minors, whatever they could get.

But the road of life has many detours.

THEY PARKED THEIR CAR IN a parking lot. They walked to the apartment through the lobby. Each was carrying a bag. George walked in front and Foster two steps behind. He took out a bunch of keys. Foster, eyes on the people that surrounded him, was being careful. Falling into a trap was one of the things he had to look out for; anything was possible with George around. They stepped into the flat and slammed the door behind them.

"The detectives might be onto us," said Foster.

George opened up a bag with cash stashed inside in bundles. They looked like stacks of two hundreds. That did not bring joy to George's face. As he put the stacks onto the table, he was looking for something. "*Something had been left out*!" he said.

Foster questioned George's actions. At last George placed his hand right inside the bag; that is when he felt a small leather pocket in the bag. He held it tight, trying to feel its contents. For all the trouble he had got himself into, this was the reason why. Foster was startled by George's face, now wreathed with a smile. It made him suspect there was something worth more than the money that was on the table. Suspicious movements were made between them. George then said to Foster, "You can take all the money on the table; this is what I came here for".

DETECTIVE MDUDUZI GAVE A SPEECH, reporting to the news team that was broadcasting on a live channel. After a while of going through the daily paper in his office, there was a knock on his office door.

"Come in." Joey was on the door. He walked right through with a brown folder in his hands. With it there was another long envelope on the side. They shook hands with happy smiles on their faces. "There is nothing as good as living an office life like this one. It is easy to get by," Detective Mduduzi said.

Joey's voice carried an accent of another language. He joined the conversation. "I have been waiting for your folder for more than three hours now. I think we have a copycat of our six-year-old trial." And then, after a short pause, "George is in town."

Mduduzi sat down and listened. Surely this cannot happen twice in a decade, although nothing is impossible these days. Even with all the data they were holding, nothing was coming out of it. Joey was not startled; he knew what was happening. However, Joey knew more about this crime than everyone else. Combining the evidence was what the detective had in mind, with the hope of a successful investigation, but it was not going to be as easy as it seemed.

Petrus Mduduzi passed on the evidence that he had gone through over the whole morning to Joey. "The story of the decade." They both laughed at the matter. As they were going through the papers, they were looking for possible similarities, some of which were there in open sight. Because of the fact that the same gun was used as before, they had to know where to start the search from. They had the idea that they were working with a lunatic, who would smile as he watched their skulls being crushed: a doomsday.

Joey started mentioning his thoughts based on true facts, although he lied about his assumptions and what he was looking at. "So, actually, he made everyone believe that a young boy did this?" he asked. "Let's try to keep it in that way. We know that he once used the same trick, and a few hours later the boy was a victim."

Joey decide to keep it decent. From what they had, they only lacked the evidence of the boy's description; they could only hope to see a dead body after few hours. It was likely that somebody was going to be shot by a bullet that he'd bought. As is so often the case, today's most wanted was the next day's victim.

"It could happen in that way," Joey suggested, "since the same thing once happened before. We might have a new victim on our hands. Because it was dark, nobody among the witnesses was able to give an exact description of the boy and it could be a little bit difficult to depend on the old woman's estimations. We might spend time on the wrong informants."

Back when Tinashe was once caught shoplifting with his accomplices, the Indian owner of the store had only scared them away. They knew he was not going to hurt them; they were used to such stores. It was possible to find piece jobs – maybe cleaning cars, passing people flyers or standing by the road and helping car parkers for a tip. This gave them enough money to buy the cannabis they needed for that time, just to get high.

Living in these streets turned Tinashe into a man before his time. At the young age of eleven he was already drinking, fantasising about women at every chance he could get, only wishing that he could have them all for himself, like a young Solomon. Minor crimes became his new jobs; he could not turn down any offer. It was not just an offer, but the ticket to better his kind of life. It was a way of making a living.

What Foster and George had for him could have been a lifetime meal ticket. His stomach was empty and stealing somebody's food to feed it was sending a message: what is good enough for you, is also good enough for me. And he had his mind made up in that way. He always had been that child who saw new sneakers, wishing he could buy them with cash.

A city filled with uncontrollable guns and violence does not exist only in the movies. Many groups around were recruiting desperate young boys into drug dealing. Tinashe had run away from his hometown, where he had been involved with a clique of that sort. He had a tattoo of a gun on his right hand; it had a greater meaning than how beautiful it was suppose to look. Days are dangerous, be hustlers and drug pushers, and when one of them raises a head to look up, who was looking out for them? No one was. Being threatened or being hurt was possible. Nobody showed any care. As long as the money was coming in, they were sure to put themselves first.

Tinashe ended up running away with the same drugs he was supposed to sell. He had adapted to a drug and prostitution environment and the environment had groomed him well.

THE BAGS SAT ON A glass table while George was going through them. He pulled out a gun. He knew more about the packages than his accomplices did. This was not just some luck in a game of coincidence. His gun was a Korth sport revolver with 152 mm barrel and micrometre sight. It had once been found at a murder scene. They are rare to find, and it looked like combat as it pointed at Foster.

Foster had a Colt Anaconda revolver. He was not fast enough, and he only stood in silence – two men in a small room. George thought of taking everything: he was greedy and sought power.

"I'd rather keep you out of this!" George was the first to say something.

"Keep me out of this?" Foster asked harsh, his face furious. "Give me what belongs to me," he added. It turned into a short conversation ("You are crazy, George"). They both stood ready to blow each other away. They had no agreement between them.

Foster said, "I know where your son is," withdrawing his gun hanging on his belt.

He was shot unaware and jumped behind a couch in the room, stumbled to the door and opened it. He started firing back, although he missed, and that gave him away. George was in the kitchen hiding noiselessly. Foster ran away without any money. *"A lunatic,"* he thought. He made it to his car with a bullet in his shoulder, while George waited soundlessly for more than two minutes in the kitchen.

He checked if Foster had run away, but he knew he had to let him go, especially if it were possible to find his son through him. Moreover, the next move was predictable. He did not regret letting him go. He went back into the lounge, finding that one bullet had gone through one of the bags. It was not a human heart that he had to be careful with, and he picked it up. He placed the gun in the bag promptly. Minutes later, the police arrived, after neighbours had reported the sounds of gunshots.

Foster drove faster, fleeing for his life, and revving up the speed. He was still bleeding. He covered the injured shoulder with a jacket while speeding to the closest pharmacy. Going in there, he only wanted a first aid kit. He paid them very fast with sweat all over his face, and as soon as he was done was back in his car, rapidly using the road they had driven on their way to the apartment. He made sure nobody was following and then it took him a few minutes to treat himself with what was in the first aid kit.

Tinashe was walking along the road sideways. He saw Foster's car coming down hard, and it was already closer than a blink of an eye. "*Death is back again,*" he thought. He stood in an open area. There was nowhere to run to and he only had to lose fear. Amazingly, Foster noticed Tinashe and stopped the vehicle at a distance before coming in more closely, as if he were going to scare him away.

Tinashe remained firm, watching the car slowing down on the other side of the same road. It scared everything out of him, and he was not looking forward to meeting George quite yet. Foster got out of the car and Tinashe noticed that something was not right. Even thought it was a scary moment, he walked over.

Foster saw Tinashe approaching and was startled again by his courage. "*Tinashe the brave one.*" He gave him that thought. He knew what to expect now: he had run into a troublemaker. Tinashe crossed the road looking better than Foster. Something had changed. He balanced against the car. He wanted to explain the foul play they'd got themselves involved in, and he got his chance.

Tinashe had chilled out, and slowly he stepped closer. Foster was looking straight into his eyes, and he looked as calm as ever. "He shot me," he said, opening his jacket. Tinashe jumped back at once: the movement scared him away. "Relax," said Foster, opening his jacket further. He was covered in blood.

It brought Tinashe close to him. He felt pity for the man, and he asked, "He shot you? Let us go." They went to the car together. Foster asked Tinashe if he could drive and Tinashe replied, "I could try".

"Where to?" Tinashe asked, and Foster thought about the hospital, but police clearance for gun wounds was a policy there. "Just to my apartment," he said and right away they left.

DETECTIVE MDUDUZI WAS URGED TO go through the evidence again and it got him busy. One of the officers to whom Detective delegated much of his work at times, knocked on the door. It seemed as if there was an emergency because he knocked quickly and loudly. "Come in," he called. Before he had a chance to speak, the officer said, "Sir, sir," repeatedly and finally added, "there is another shooting down at ZHC apartments. We might find something there." Petrus got up from his chair and grabbed his jacket. Mduduzi and Joey Morish pulled themselves together and walked out of the office, going to the scene. "Let's hurry," Morish urged. The weather was becoming chilly.

Petrus had a Ford from about seven years ago, but it was still new in his eyes. Joey remembered it well. "You are still loaded with this monster of yours," Joey said. They both laughed.

"I have always referred to that car as my second-born child." A smile was the only thing that the detective would have whenever he looked at that Ford, no matter how sad the day had been. Then he said, "Of course it is," like he had forgotten to answer that question earlier on.

GEORGE HAD A SCAR ON his face, it was not too big, and neither was it too small. It was just the right size to be noticeable and mentioned in any statement. The evidence extracted from all the interviews did not mention anything about a man with face scar, but Joey knew that this was the same man, surely. He had strong instincts or perhaps the mathematics was just too obvious: in his mind the equation was solved.

The two investigators drove to the new crime scene discussing any possibility that might change the whole point of view between the new case and a previous one.

Chapter 2

"So I was supposed to be dead now," Tinashe mumbled to Foster.

Foster decided to add his own sorrow to that. "And me too," Foster said in a low voice, alerting Tinashe that he was not the only one with the fear of death.

"Why did you then shoot me instead of him? We could have taken the whole thing for ourselves," he asked in search of an answer, and there was nothing that Foster could say so he shut his mouth and let Tinashe figure it out for himself. Tinashe was no longer shivering in fear.

After a while, Foster answered Tinashe's question. "You were supposed to be terminated after retrieving the bags. I decide to put it into my consideration." He stopped for a second, and checked to see if he had stopped bleeding. Foster told Tinashe the truth that hurt him for that minute. He said, "George was furious that I did not kill you the moment we robbed the bags."

Tinashe pulled over onto the roadside, anger crossing him. For some reason he projected his insecurities onto other people and he was dancing with the devil. He asked, "What will stop you from killing me later, when you are home safe?"

Foster made his own suggestion. "Why did I not do it before? Alternatively, do I have to regret sparing your life, boy?" Questions without any suitable answers are profound. Again, he thought about making his way to a hospital. They exchanged seats and Foster drove to a hospital that was only five minutes away. When they were at the hospital, Tinashe remained seated in the car. Foster hoped to find the boy still in the car when he got back.

He approached a receptionist and a nurse near-by came closer to look. She had seen the red stains on his shirt and realised he needed help very fast. "Is it a gun wound?" she asked jokingly, and seriously Foster answered, "Yes, it is," but she thought it was sarcasm. Then she realised that he was serious and her smile faded away like a flower. "We only treat these wounds with a police clearance and an insurance plan in hand, otherwise, I am sorry, we cannot help," she said.

Down at the car park, something was going on. An ambulance came and parked next to Foster's car and its driver got out. Quickly, Foster walked out of the hospital with an untreated wound. His head for a while was not okay, mentally.

Tinashe had an idea. Foster took it and implemented it that second. They were able to get something that was going to help Foster's shoulder. Foster could not have done it as fast as the boy did it. After snooping into the ambulance and snatching out every piece of aid he could see, he placed them next to him in the back seat. They drove away from the hospital, making their way to a safe place. Nursing himself was now Foster's first priority. It was a sad joke.

JOEY AND PETRUS REACHED THEIR destination at the ZHC apartments. Officers were collecting anything they could find. A bad thing was that a drunkard was the only witness to what had happened. Even with blood splattering the wall and a couple of used bullets lying around, they would not necessarily find something they could actually use. Joey and Petrus went inside the apartment where George and Foster had exchanged bullets.

Joey could smell their fragrances like a sniffing dog, and what he saw stunned him as much as it had everyone else. His confidence that it was a related case took a knock; it looked like a gangster playground for a couple of amateurs. At first glance it did not look related. Then he picked up a little piece of money, and his confidence built up again.

Petrus on the other hand had collected blood samples, which he had better use for. They walked away from the scene, laughing about unrelated matters. "Maybe we can go down to the head office for the DNA test of these samples I got," said Petrus.

MAKING SURE THAT THEY WERE not being followed, Tinashe kept his eyes on the rear view mirror and Foster kept his on the road. "Fosse, what is the main plan, if you really do have one?" Tinashe asked, just to make sure that a future around Foster was certain. He had regularly called him *Fosse*. There was a moment of silence between them. "Where are we going to now?" He asked many questions, and this one created another boring silence.

"You ask too many questions for a boy of your age, Tinashe." To Foster, it felt like a burden being around Tinashe. His engine revved loudly. Foster leaned back, striving to drive slowly. He drove down north to get where he was going as quickly as possible.

TWO POLICEMEN WENT TO THE hospital. After a silly report came in, and they'd even made a joke out of it, it was reported again, so they went to check it out. They laughed that someone had stolen the paramedics' supplies.

Essential time was not wasted. Everything was on security tape, including a copy of footage that had a small part of a boy sneaking from one car to another. The picture and the camera angle was distorted. They did not pay much attention until they went to the computer control room although they were aware that someone does not just steal a paramedic kit for nothing.

They all agreed to see the original copy of the footage so the two police officers walked to the control room with one of the hospital security officers. When they walked into the hospital, they used one of the private entrances that can only lead into the first floor hallway.

It was so bright that the dark spots could not find anywhere to start a family. Three doors down the hallway was the control room. The guard produced a key and opened the door, murmuring, "After you".

The police officers followed him into the room with more CCTV than that of a prison playground. They both stood back, and he started entering passwords to establish himself as the current user. Within the blink of an eye he was into the system and already rewinding to previous hours and activities that had occurred in the garage.

"You might wait a few minutes while I run this slow process, Officers," said the guard. In no time both officers stepped forward as they had their eyes on a simple action that had occurred in that garage. It showed exactly what had happened: how Foster went to the car, how Tinashe came out, taking all the meds that were useful to Foster. One of the police officers questioned himself: "*Why would they steal meds and the kit while coming out of the hospital? Who was coming out of the hospital into the car?*"

"Quickly," he said, "can you please rewind the whole footage to show us while he was still in the hospital." How clever and interesting it was becoming. They were starting to notice that they had an actual story in hand. The camera rolled back from the reception to when a nurse walked up to him. "Pause, this is it." Again he stopped and then continued, "Can you please zoom in on the face if possible".

When there was enough magnification to it, they noticed he was injured, probably from a gun wound, and that is why he was never treated. They wanted the clearance and an open-minded police officer. Who they failed to recognise was the boy who had actually stolen the medical supplies.

They reported everything, and the acknowledgment about gun shots occurring three to five kilometres around the CBD came in quickly.

Detective Mduduzi was in the same area. He was on his way to get DNA extracted from the samples he had. He and Joey ran into the two police officers in the hospital, but they only gave each other a nod and passed on, minding their own businesses.

TINASHE AND FOSTER WERE ALMOST at the old apartment. Tinashe was in the driver's seat and Foster sat in the back. Giving the directions was all he could do for the moment. He was anxious and there was increasing pain coming from his shoulder.

Tinashe had death following him and he did not forget about the money he had been promised. The person he'd done the crime with had his own cruel demon following him too. "If you notice that building with a stationery advertisement chart…" Tinashe noticed the building Foster mentioned and, after making a few turns, drove into the garage. The two accomplices got out of the car and locked its doors. Tinashe carried the first aid kit bag into the building.

"THIS TIME WE CANNOT LET him slip through our fingers like water. Fool me once and shame on you, but fool me twice, shame on me." The truth for Joey was this: he was not going to lose to George, although George's involvement in all this was still only a theory.

Detective Mduduzi urged him, "From the evidence retrieved in the morning, the bullets were from which gun?" He tried to remember, so that he could tell Joey, who was holding a paper file with a photo attached to it.

Joey asked, "Which gun is it?" Luckily, the detective remembered which one it was and Joey remembered the bullets. "It is the same one from years ago, apparently. Yeah, oh! It is." It all became clear in a moment of enlightenment.

They wanted to reach one of the private facilities they only named *The Department*. They'd seen Foster's face and recognised it on the CCTV footage recorded in the hospital garage. Dr Choo had told them about the short series of events that had occurred in the hospital. After that, he'd told them about how they would get help faster at *The Department* than at the hospital.

Foster and Tinashe sat quietly in the apartment. They were both wondering why they were still in the same room, broke. Tinashe had allegations against Foster but he dropped his pride after having been saved twice. Foster had allegations against George, and in his mind it was a blood bath.

"Who do you live with?" Tinashe asked and Foster looked him directly in the eye.

"Why are you asking? Did you notice anything unusual?"

"No! No," he replied with a surprised look, although he had certainly noticed something.

"I do not like company," he said, and hopefully Tinashe understood. "What about you?" Foster asked with curiosity.

"With God," answered Tinashe, making like it was a joke, although he only had a little laugh and a smile.

"You should come and live here. It seems you have been living in the streets for some time now," Foster told him on a serious note and he then encouraged him to think about it.

Making a decision "yes or no" is easy, but to live up to it is hard. On balance, it was a better choice to stay because he had nothing to lose. However, Tinashe said, "No, I'd rather stick to where my purpose is. It suits me well there, if you know what I mean." Without any arguments Foster agreed.

Every time Foster dug down into Tinashe's soul, he saw infinite potential and it was not a debatable matter. "If you want some food," he stood up while talking, "you can prepare some for yourself in the kitchen".

It was not a shame for him, although he knew nothing about cooking and he had just been given permission to play around with it. His stomach was empty and this was the first time in his life that he'd walked into a proper kitchen. Foster sat down again as if he had forgotten something, and then he stretched his other hand out to reach for the remote control. He started increasing the music sound. Tinashe stood at the microwave, trying to figure out how to use it

"ALMOST THERE," MDUDUZI SAID TO Joey. He slowed and turned into a car park that had grey tents covering each car. He found a space where his Ford could fit properly.

"By the way…" Joey dragged his words, "last time…" He continued as if he were not sure of what to say exactly, or as if what he had in mind was still just thoughts. Again he said, "By the way, last time, remember a boy was one of the victims… same old trick. Have you heard any report about any dead boy?"

"Not yet, Joey," Petrus replied.

"This time it is a whole different operation. I think something went down. Wrong or right, we will have to find out for ourselves."

They walked straight into the room that they had been told to go to. It was well equipped with large and small equipment. They shook hands with a Doctor Stevens, whom they had called earlier, after Choo had given them his direct line.

"Give me the sample," he said as soon as they were done with greetings. "This may take a while and, if not, then the person is well known to your database." Then he started doing what he was best at. The detective and sergeant were offered a seat. Joey went on to sit down but whenever Petrus got the chance to stand up straight, he indulged it properly. One of the assistants came over to them, offering them something to drink, but neither were thirsty. Joey pulled out his phone and started going through it.

The doctor kept on shaking the sample in a small tube where he had mixed it with another compound. He put some droplets onto his machines and continued testing them. Stevens printed out the DNA profile as Detective Mduduzi and Joey stood a few metres away. The former had his body leaned against the wall next to a big shelf cupboard, while Joey sat on a well designed brown bench. They were both rehashing stories not yet told, stories of the past, catching up.

After thirty minutes the data had been fed into the computer database, and a name had been recognised through the DNA sample. "Thanks, Stevens, I owe you one." The detective walked to him, the smile he gave coming from the inside gums of his mouth, showing his gleaming white teeth.

"Here is the memory stick with the information and I have sent an image to your phone." Quickly, he pulled out his phone and he opened the new message. When he opened it, he was not shocked. He put the stick into his inside jacket pocket. Business as usual, that is all that it was.

He said, "We have what we came for, let's proceed." With wide smiles, they left.

A Ford Ranger was coming out of the medical research facility car park, facing the front main gate which was painted black and white. The gate opened up moving in separate directions, breaking from the middle. Petrus' intentions were to go back to the office but, before they took their path back to the office, Joey insisted on paying the bill if they just dropped by a restaurant. He kept on suggesting that it was time to fill up their empty stomachs.

"Who would have thought you were going to marry Anna at some point in life?" Joey asked. Detective Mduduzi gave a laugh of joy and embraced the happiness that God had given him, which included Anna and his children.

"Oh yeah, even me, I did not think so myself," he replied and it was just left as a story for another day. Joey had an extra thought and point of view that was different from all the usual. It seemed like he knew something that nobody else did; that some unspeakable story kept him quiet.

They parked in front of a restaurant. The restaurant had square brown tables and chairs that were well arranged. Two tables were laid outside next to the door, and they went and sat down at one of them. A waitress had already begun her services. She was light in complexion and in her late twenties. She offered them something to drink and they both agreed to water with ice and lemon. She gave them a great smile and with it she had given them an obligation to give her a tip.

She came back from the counter, holding a black tray with two water glasses in her hands. Petrus and Joey were looking through the menu. “Good people,” she said, “we have some specials this evening which you might care to try?”

“I will stick to the menu.” Joey made it easy for himself as he had found something he liked on the menu.

“Same here.” The detective remained cool.

Ten minutes later, she walked to their table with two oval platters and placed them on the table. Each side had its cutlery and the exact food that they had ordered. “Please enjoy,” she said, and she left the two men revelling in their meal.

“It is now six o’clock.” Joey looked at his watch. Empty stomachs were filled with good food, leaving the platters empty. They were ready to leave and Joey waved his hand to the waitress. She came and collected the platters, they paid the bill, and left. They would go back to the office where they would have to work harder than anticipated. Patience runs out when needed the most, and Joey felt restless as the results were nothing but trouble.

Petrus drove and, with nothing else to discuss, he pulled out an envelope that had some files placed together as evidence. The evidence was for him to see, but he was stuck with Joey, and sharing information might bring light at the end of the tunnel. He struggled to get information from him, so he shared what he had with Joey.

Joey kept on flipping the pages in the folder file, as if he were looking for some sort of information that he’d missed while going through them before. He finally stopped at a picture at the centre of an A4-sized piece of paper, and he kept on staring at it. He wanted to know the meaning beneath and beyond the paper; the picture he focused on reminded him of something. Joey’s left hand moved around the picture.

“We are here. Let’s move one step forward.” Petrus locked the car and they went into the office, where they went to the computer in Petrus’ office and put the flash drive into the USB slot. When the files was opened, their eyes were drawn to the name that appeared: Stanley Ncube aka Foster, the name he'd eared during his incarceration. More information was displayed below the name and curiosity made them read it faster. Nothing could have taken their attention away from that time. As they scrolled down, a full quality face picture appeared. "Perhaps he is the killer," Joey told the detective with first-hand analysis.

"Let's review more about him."

Stanley Ncube, also known as Foster, had been arrested a few times and had appeared in court several times. Once he had been thrown behind bars. "He is clean but dirty," Joey said. "He has managed to stay clean all this time, why this now?"

"I think I know where to find Mr Stanley," said Detective Mduduzi.

TINASHE AND FOSTER HAD JUST finished up their meal. Foster had seen the struggle happening in the kitchen and he'd decided to extend his one hand, the only hand that was still in use for the time being. His hatred of medication was not helping. He'd avoided taking a shower that would end up affecting his shoulder bandages and he could not take out the bullet because the process carried to much suffering. He tried to embrace its pain but it looked like it had become infected. No way was the first aid kit going to stop that infection. He needed medical assistance quickly. He had spent the whole day with an untreated wound, and it was now at a point where a specialist was required.

He urged Tinashe to take a bath. Still wearing his black vest, Tinashe right away went to the shower. A few minutes later, somebody knocked on the door twice, heavy knocks that gave him thoughts of George. "*This does not happen often,*" Foster thought. He picked up his gun and walked to the door. Peeking through the key hole, he saw a jacket only; that was someone else, not George.

Two men were standing outside. He opened the door, ready to shoot with the gun hidden behind his back. Detective Mduduzi and Joey waited to see Mr Stanley Ncube. Luckily the table was clean of the armoury, and before either of them had noticed the gun in his hand, he had forced it to hang at his waist. He wanted to keep it where he could reach it. He had worn a T-shirt over his vest.

"You are not a very hard man to find, Foster" said the detective.

"Why should I be a hard one?" Foster replied with a crocodile smile.

He invited the two gentleman to come in. He knew they had come to talk which meant they wanted something first, otherwise they would have come with a convoy and would have come in, even without permission.

"Where were you the whole day?" Joey asked with an expression formed in eyes that could not settle at one place.

Foster calmly answered, "I was home all day."

Tinashe was done with a quick shower when he heard voices coming from the sitting room. They had sat down but, just to be careful, Joey kept his eyes on his gun and Foster's hands. Tinashe was eavesdropping from a distance, making sure he went unnoticed.

"Hiding yourself from the public, huh?" Joey with a certain smile mumbled aloud and a new look had humour in it. They were both sitting in a couch with a gun beneath it. Stanley was sitting in a far corner. Questions kept on coming at him; they were setting up an exam for him.

"So, would you mind elaborating on what is going on, Foster?" The detective did not want to go any further by trying to be too hardcore.

"Why the hell are you chilling at home at this hour?" Petrus asked, raising his right hand showing his gold wristwatch to him. Meanwhile, Joey showed anger, fierceness and curiosity, as patience ran out for him like a victim's breath. His was more the military police attitude.

Joey said, “You are bleeding”.

“Where?” Foster asked, as if it were a surprise. He was beginning to feel agitated; he thought he had sorted it out.

“That shoulder, right there.” Joey pointed his finger to Foster’s wounded shoulder. “It needs to be fixed while it’s still possible, otherwise you might need to start making some calls so that you can get it replaced.” Joey brought some sarcasm into the picture. He lifted his leg onto the table top, just to provoke Foster, but Foster let it slide by ignoring it.

“So, should we go to the station to take down some details and charge you with armed robbery?” Joey asked, adding that the charges were serious and beginning to itemise the evidence that they had.

Foster sat in the corner scared more than ever. He was looking at more than two decades in prison. But Stanley remained calm and asked, a slightly higher note in his voice, “What are you two bragging about?”

“I am saying that we have your video that shows you while you were stealing your so called first aid kit and, added to that, we found your blood messed in an apartment rented out to an unknown man and paid for with cash.”

All this sounded serious to the ears of Tinashe. The charges were starting to get serious.

“Do you have any conclusions?”

“Not yet,” said Joey. “But I am sure that you will not be sleeping in your bed tonight.” Joey told him this so that they could come to an understanding.

A guilty look crossed Stanley’s face. He wanted the fierceness of a lion, to walk like a lion and roar like one, but they had him in a corner.

“By the way, where is the boy you were with earlier in the morning, or maybe the whole day?” Petrus asked. The chance had come up for Stanley to explain himself and maybe to offer them a deal that would not just get him out of going behind bars but may get him out of it rich. That was what they were looking for.

"We will leave with you now because we do not have the whole day," Joey said. Foster knew that these man did not want a bribe; they actually wanted what he wanted, and the enemy of my enemy is my friend. Joey continued speaking. "Plus your body is getting cold, that thing you have on your shoulder takes time to patch up." His time was running out and he had to think fast before they did for him.

"Where is the body? Where did you bury the boy?"

Foster would have liked to answer all these question but the pain he felt made him feel like he wanted to rip his arm off. For that moment his focus continued on the pain. His body was getting colder, as if it were freezing actually. He gave a small laugh before he answered. "Business as usual," he said, making the situation simple. "*We have our differences,*" he thought, "*but a collaboration would be beneficial*". Outright war was too expensive for him to afford, especially in this situation. His energy had left and here was an opportunity to regain it.

"The boy is still alive," he said. "*I have worked with him and he's marvellous,*" he thought, "*and this time he was carrying large.*"

The detective opened up the air. "Something went right this time," Detective Mduduzi said. He was shocked, as all the missions that George had carried out previously had failed.

The men sat and discussed the fall of another. A deal was made. When such alliances are made, that is when a sheep wears a wolf's mask, and a partnership has to stand and make changes accordingly. Foster promised to light their investigation a little further. For them, he was not the answer, and they had to cut a deal.

The two policemen told him to meet them the next day at a place called Dikoto Dia Mall. "I know it," he answered as they left the room. Without any goodbyes, they went out into the passage and found their way to the lift.

Stanley was left behind with the look of a man who has been betrayed by his cheating wife, on his own bed that he bought himself. The men had left him a contact for Doctor Choo, so that he could get his wound patched up, and once they were out of the way Foster stood up and Tinashe ran back into the bathroom. Foster saw him coming out of the bathroom and assumed that that meant that he had not heard a thing.

There was a refrigerator that was used to cover a space that existed between the sitting room and kitchen and ran all the way to the bathroom. It would be a hiding place for Tinashe. Facing the front, he grabbed his keys and Tinashe walked up to him. In a loud voice Foster said “Stay here! And wait here. Whoever knocks on the door, do not open, otherwise I will find you dead here.” Closing the door behind him, he looked warily into the passage, for he now feared for his own life.

Tinashe was left sitting on the couch watching music videos. Foster had never really liked the set. He’d only bought it for guests such as Tinashe. He avoided watching programs and commercials that assaulted him with a rapid succession of images. Not knowing what else to do, Tinashe sat right there. It might take Foster two hours or so, so he decided to relax but his mind would not. He was trying to analyse each and every word that he’d heard. He had just sat right where Joey Morish had recently been sitting.

He stared at the television for many minutes. Then he thought of a way out but he highly doubted that it could be successful. After thirty minutes, his eyes were as tired as his body. He could barely open his eyes; the lids felt so heavy that he could not keep on lifting them up.

A couple of hours later, Foster came back. Hearing footsteps, Tinashe woke up right away, opening his eyes wide quickly to see who it was, using his hand to wipe away the sleep. He relaxed visibly when he saw Foster.

"Relax," Foster said. He did not say anything else. He held a plastic bag in his hand and in the other a pack of cigarettes. He walked to his bedroom.

AFTER LEAVING THE APARTMENT, THE detective's phone kept on ringing. Each time he answered, few words were said. Most of his calls were only a quick chat; longer than that usually meant a family matter. He believed that in his line of work a conversation can be recorded easily.

"That was Anna that I just got off on the phone with. She said she has prepared a guest room for you." The detective laughed as he told Joey about this. "She will appreciate it if you come along with me and spend a night at my house," he added. They made their way to his house.

WHEN FOSTER WALKED INTO HIS bedroom, he remembered the shopping bag. He grabbed a blanket. He had seen Tinashe's hands wrapped around each other and the pain he'd felt in his shoulder wound was the same he felt for the boy without a blanket. Although, he thought, another problem had just walked into his life in the form of the two gentlemen who had left the apartment two hours back.

After he'd given the blanket to the boy, who was to sleep on the couch, Stanley went to lie on top of his bed that was covered with brown sheets. His thoughts travelled miles away. He though of just getting out of this, of opening his eyes and it would all have disappeared. "*Superman,*" he thought.

WHEN THEY REACHED HIS HOUSE, and the car had been parked straight into the garage, Petrus and Joey used the garage door into the house. "How are you, my love?" his wife asked as Petrus entered the kitchen, and then asked how work was. Then she asked where Joey was. At that point, Joey walked into the house as if he owned it. He had a wide grin on his face.

No one knew the exact words to say that would not ruin the moment. Everyone had happy faces and there were more smiley faces from the kids. Anna asked, “How have you been? The last time I heard about you was about seven years back.”

Joey and Petrus’ friendship had formed after doing a couple of jobs together and once upon time they had the worked on a case involving George. They all sat on kitchen chairs varnished in white. It was like one of those daily television show dramas you could find in every city. Petrus grabbed two cold bottles, “non-alcoholic”, out of the fridge. For the moment, they put work aside. Joey shared jokes with the kids. Petrus’ son Thapiso had just turned seven about two weeks back, and he told Uncle Joey all his stories.

The night was at its peak point and then good nights were said and everyone went off to bed. But when the dreams had begun in Petrus’ house, somebody else was up.

GEORGE SPENT HIS HALF-DAY SLEEPING after making a series of serious troubles. He had paid a hotel with cash. It was not five stars but just one of those average, well maintained ones, and he had quietly paid just to stay for a certain time there. Now the time was up. His eyes were on the bags. After he had searched a bag thoroughly, he’d found a memory stick inside one of those black leather pockets that had diamonds in them.

George had a face scar – they called it a war scar – but you could not identify it from a distance, and, wearing a coat that reached his thighs, he was on the threshold of completing a dazzling mission. He wore original army boots. His eyes were sometimes red. At six foot, he was a little above average height. His health had deteriorated due to living in prison conditions for some years, but now he was as strong as ever.

A car waited for him outside. He had called a meter taxi and it was a white Toyota with its driver ready to take off. George’s eyes were on the phone, checking the number plate. He boarded and the tyres started rolling slowly. They almost ran into a red robot, but he kept quiet in the back seat of the car. He wanted to go to a club and he had given the directions to the taxi driver.

SF Club House was a name everybody knew. He remembered one thing: that the owner of the place, Zhen, held no jokes. He was holding a large amount of treasure and that meant increased bills. He had to go to that one place.

But first he needed the taxi driver to take him to a bank that had 24/7 services. Not everyone would have expected that he would leave his spoils in a bank, but he knew one thing and one thing only: if he lost them, he was going to be eaten alive if caught.

The dark had covered the city. The car's inside lights were off, and there were just the rhythms of the engine. He was hoping to get a good exchange rate from these boys.

SERGEANT JOEY WAS ON THE phone, taking a call in the guest room. At that moment he looked relaxed and less worried. "How are you?" he said on the phone. A woman's voice answered, "Exhausted. Is your work coming along alright? When are you expecting to come back home? I miss you." She really had missed him. Joey smiled and remembered how much she loved him. That was his wife, Lisa. After many years of trying, Lisa had eventually fallen pregnant, and the couple were waiting in anticipation for the birth.

The call lasted about six minutes, enough for them to exchange a part of their life that they were not sharing at that particular moment. They felt the need to fill up the empty gaps between them.

AT THE BANK, GEORGE HAD been given a number and password. He was now only left with enough cash in his pocket to support his needs for that time. It was still a lot, and he carried it in a brown envelope. When the taxi got to the club, a lot of cars were parked outside. It seemed as if there was already an ongoing function, and he did not know if he would be welcomed. It had been a long time since he'd visited the place.

The taxi driver was looking out for a space to park. "I highly doubt I'll find one," he said and pulled over on the side road so that George could get out there. He approached the club's front door. Two big security officers stood there. They both covered the entrance. A line of young people trying to gain entrance into the club – each holding quite expensive tickets – was formed against the wall. At that time of the year the clubs would be homes for many, as the students were done with exams.

George reached the security people and he saw that they had noticed him and thought that probably they were just going to take him as one of the commoners. However, he had questions coming for him. They had eyes on him already, "Can I help you?" one of the men asked. George only told him that he was a friend of Zheng, the club owner. It was strictly business; he was not a common visitor.

One of the guards left the post to accompany George. Another one replaced him. He gave them a name and identification card that corresponded to the details. While people were still fighting to get past the security officers, they opened a way for him and he walked down the stairs.

The Buyers

GEORGE WALKED INTO THE VIP section. It was a well designed room with a very big fish tank that separated the room from the public sections. The security guard who had accompanied him returned to his post and another one took George inside. George had a face that looked as if he did not want to be bothered. The club was filled with many young people, and those who noticed him thought he was too old for this partying thing – and they were correct – but he was all about the money.

George was taken to Zhen, who recognised him as he walked in. Zhen had a grinning face. He bowed his head as a sign of greeting and respect. George and Zhen had done a lot of business. George brought a lot of deals to Zhen and for that reason he was welcomed, but he was never to think for a second that he had Zhen in the palm of his hand, because that would turn out messier than planned. He offered George a drink which was gladly accepted, and they joined the crew. It seemed like old friends were back on the same path and that is life.

"Tell me George, what do you have for me?" Zhen quickly asked.

George replied, "Why are you in such a hurry?" Music could be heard in the background.

"A few people have been coming around and I heard the sergeant is back in town."

"Your ears are still working properly, I can see. I might need to use them sometime during the coming days." George wanted a favour, and surely Zhen understood that a friend in need is a friend indeed.

They laughed when George heard that the empire that was once a paradise of Eden was in big trouble; he knew the exact meaning of it. Although one of Zhen's people, almost his closest friend, had never really liked George, Zhen thought George was just a guy who needed somebody to shine light on him, and he was the one who was going to do it. George did not have any fear of death in him, light was no longer shining on his soul.

After George had given Zhen his business proposition, he finished his drink. He looked around to see if he was being followed, trying to cover his steps. No one was worth trusting and a friend was to be a friend only when needed. He walked away from the club and then he was in a strictly hustling zone. Worried about his safety, he jumped into a taxi that was close to him, just down the road from the club.

Chapter 3

Time was passing. Everybody wanted answers but no-one could have all of them in time. Some did not have questions yet; they only had high expectations of what was to come. Foster's dreams were running away before his eyes. He could not fall asleep. He tried falling asleep but he could not dream. His position of feeling crucified after losing his power, was eating his soul. His thoughts only said, *"How can I come out clean in this?"*

During that night, he opened his eyes wide open, stretching the muscles and wondering how to get out of this. He'd got himself in, and was well determined to get himself out again by any means. He never lost the first impression of the first visit. If he was going to be buried anytime soon, his grave would be next to that of his enemies by means of revenge. But when revenge graves are dug, they are dug in twos. He knew the time was going to come when his help was no longer of importance.

Around three in the morning he woke up. He did not sleep that long and this was not good for his health. Slowly he got off the bed. If he moved too quickly, his shoulder would disagree. He walked through the room that Tinashe was sleeping in and into the kitchen, opening up the fridge to grab something to eat. It was so quiet; the no sounds of an overwhelming muddle of hooting and shouting being carried by the wind. Most people were asleep although probably a few like him were still awake. They were not facing common problems and it was either serious business or go to sleep.

Thoughts of his cousin Jadea ran through his mind as he walked back to his bedroom, holding a bottle of water. He grabbed another blanket for Tinashe and covered the boy. It was getting cold, he felt, although maybe it was just his cold shoulder.

Jadea had a reputation of messing things up, especially when someone had given him high hopes, but he was feared by most. They said he could sometimes be over vigorous. Foster grabbed his phone, which he had placed on top of a small table in the shape of the Eiffel Tower that was next to his bed. He sat on his bed and switched on the lamp. He started going through the phone applications and contacts, searching for a number that was a direct line to get to Jadea right away. He found his number and called him, but unfortunately it was not answered. He dialled three times. Then, at last, as he was placing his phone back on the table top, a call came through. "Hello."

"Shoo, bro, why have you placed a call this time of the morning? You woke me up," Jadea said.

"Something came up, Brums," Foster said after he'd told Jadea to relax and that sleeping does not pay the bills.

"I am listening." Jadea started taking heed.

"I was shot yesterday and I am lucky that I survived because that shooter does not miss."

"Who is the fool?" Jadea's anger was provoked by this. "Who did that to you?"

"It was that army guy you once saw me with, but I have something more precious than the bullet he has put in my shoulder," Foster said. "He gave me a call one week ago, talking about that old job. Easy one I thought, and for sure it was, but I was not fully aware of him being the most difficult part of the job. We did the job and the fool needed to take everything, so he played us."

"Us! How many were you?" Jadea asked.

"Three. Me and him and the little fella who I am with now. He even wanted the both of us dead. I believe the boy might be his son and he almost killed him. He actually wanted us dead after the job was done, although the boy made it perfect."

Foster then asked Jadea if he would come over. "I will explain when you get here," he said. Jadea told Foster that within hours they would be working on a permanent solution. Foster knew that whatever Jadea said he would do, the results usually related to his words.

He woke Tinashe who quickly opened his eyes.

SOME HAD SLEPT EARLY ON at the detective's house. Anna had however woken and gone to the kitchen. When she came back to the bedroom, she slipped quietly back under the blanket next to Petrus. She laid down slowly and closely to Petrus. She tried not to wake him up but once he felt her cold hands on his back he woke up. The love between them remained invincible.

When she was in the kitchen, she'd ran into Joey and they had not had a generous conversation. Now, the detective and his wife were trying to discuss whatever was going on in their life and she was scared for his life, as she once had had an experience with George, whom her husband hated so much. He had only told her that it was the same old story, and then he'd thought about just telling her half of the story.

"A place was once hit when you were pregnant with Thapiso," he said.

"A place was hit, what do you mean by hit? I do not understand," she said.

"I only know that high up people are involved in all these transactions among these countries. This is big," he continued. "If Joey keeps on playing around with things... I'm not certain... something is not in its proper position."

All this was Greek in her ears, but she only said, "Okay. Please, do not die. I still need you and your kids still need their father," she looked closely into his eyes and kept her mouth from asking too many question.

The Second Day

JOEY AND PETRUS WENT IN to Petrus' office early the next morning. Joey used Petrus' office to receive his necessary heads up. He stretched out to reach the long envelope lying on the table. It was a ninety-nine percent probability that the information inside the envelope belonged to him. Envelopes of that kind were rare and only specific people used them for specific work.

That morning, Detective Mduduzi wore a leather jacket that was similar to the one Foster had on. He placed it in the far corner of his office. "Did they find him?" he asked Joey while opening the curtains for more light to come in. Whenever he was at work, he considered it his second home. He could work with peace of mind. Outside his window it was a crazy and busy morning. The road was busy because it was pick up time. Taxi drivers were busy making irritating non-stop noise with their engine starters, whilst private cars of people with different lives passed by, hooting.

"Yeah, we always must remember: this is not the first time!" Joey replied. "I have his number. We can try to reach him."

There was a knock on the door and they both looked at each other as if they were expecting someone. They had high hopes that he would be the one walking in. However, It was not their friend.

A policewoman walked in. "Good morning, Detective, how is your morning?" she asked. She had her eyes on Joey, although her mouth was directed to the detective. "Detective, there is a man who is here to see you." Naalehu left and went to call the visitor. When he was ushered in, four eyes were on him. Petrus leaned back in his office chair. Foster's left arm was in sling. He was wearing a leather jacket over it, while the sling had its belts rounding up through his neck via the chest.

"So, tell me, why exactly am I here?" he asked them, after he had greeted them and they had offered him a seat, although the right question that he had in his thoughts was: *What do you have for me?* He had a lot to learn.

"Relax. We will discuss that later," Petrus said.

"You would not be here if you didn't want the same thing as us." Joey had him corned. He wanted to tell them about chemistry but they also knew a thing or two about chemistry. He was not the usual visitor and he had come to stay hoping that it would not last forever.

"We know where he is. We have his contacts… so you can help us, and we can help you. We call him and talk to him. That is as far as negotiations go. If he refuses to give up, then we will be forced to give all of it."

Joey picked up the landline, so that he could dial the number on the file. The file had a stamp of classification on it, photos with further descriptions detailing everything about their suspect. The line went through and someone picked up the phone.

"What went wrong, George? It was a simple job and everything is in sideways right now. You wanted to find your way back into the game. Would you mind explaining what went wrong?"

"There is nothing to explain. I was hanged and backstabbed by many knives. I thought you saw it coming. Why did you call?" George asked.

Joey replied, "Yes, you were betrayed at some point. Now end this and bring back the bags. All the boys recommended you to handle it and you have let them down. By the way, your boy is not dead."

It felt like they were offering him everything. But he was sure that within a week all of their heads were going to be six feet under. Everybody was scared

"Both of us will be dead after a few days if the parcel is not shared equally with the right owners. They are thinking games are being played here."

"No muss, no fuss, pick up time and place," he murmured on the phone.

Joey picked the proper place and time. They all thought they had a better understanding. The sand of sounds and feelings that were conveyed on the phone went inside, deep into George's mind. For a moment, the feeling of losing his son petrified him. He was not to trust anyone. He concentrated to pull himself together, with a deep determination that was to isolate him from others as it always did. A bump and jolt threatened to make him scatter into little pieces.

A battle had begun between him and his former colleagues. There would be no back and forth; the scene itself at first contradicted war but it was too late to go back and start over. Anything that has been done in the past, right or wrong, can never be wiped out and replaced by a different past. Nevertheless, we move on and forgive ourselves because lives are made of the present moment and the future to come. Let go of the past, because it belongs there.

It was a place to pull few tricks, enough to make someone an exemplar of greed and power when they have over stepped the mark. When visitors extend their welcome it is a game without laws and rules, and surely it is dangerous.

AT THE CORNER OF 4TH Jameson street, an expensive car made a turn and parked by one of the old buildings from the 40s, next to a hotel. Jadea was driving and Tinashe was next to him. For a long time they said nothing, although they'd seemed inseparable from the time they'd got into the car. After Jadea had said the first word, his mouth became a grenade of words and he barely kept quiet after that. The change of gearbox was subtle. Although they'd had limited conversation at first – because of the stories of their lives they could not relate – a few minutes later it was a quality conversation. The funny ended when an SMS came through while they were basting out with jokes.

"Is it from your cousin?" Tinashe wanted him to read the message out.

"Wait, let me check, young money." Jadea took his time, he entered the password – 1985. He had a little shock, but it went unnoticed even though his eyebrows shot up.

"What does it say?" Tinashe murmured. Jadea showed Tinashe the picture that had been sent in the message and the details pertaining to it.

"Do you know him?"

In a thinner voice Tinashe said, "Yeah, I know him". His response sounded like he was filled with fear.

"Okay, this is your stupid father, Tinashe."

This only brought sadness to the boy. He lowered his face and shook his head, left and right, up and down, regretting any wish he'd had about never having been born to a life full of misery; repenting whatever wish he'd ever made about having his father around. In short, this is not what he'd expected.

Although tears rarely flowed out of his eyes, at this moment they did. The man who had wanted him dead had all the time been his father. "*My Father who abandoned me before I was born and then wanted me dead when life chose to bring us together. My father is a thug,*" he thought.

Jadea for a moment had a cold feeling, putting himself into the young man's shoes. He remembered what it had been like growing up in the hands of a drunkard, his own father. He felt pity for Tinashe, but he did not have to. Soon he would realise that.

"Here, this is his number if you want to call him." Tinashe had already started imprisoning himself with thoughts and questions. *What should I say to him this time?* Without further notice, he wanted to call. That was the only way he could get answers to his infinite number of questions.

Jadea suggested that, after calling him, he might feel better and this was true, but it was one of the oldest tricks in book. They were playing George, and Tinashe would be better off without him. But

George was the one able to answer all the questions that the fourteen-year-old had.

Jadea started dialling when they had both agreed to call him. Tinashe was not to be trusted from their perceptive. He could sabotage the plan Foster had drafted. The number went through on the first dial but, after a moment of silence, the call failed. Tinashe by now was sure to say something.

Jadea gave it a second try: missed call. How to say what he wanted was bothering him. "Put it on the loud speaker." He wanted to hear whatever George had to say.

There was another call for Jadea and he changed the language while answering it. "I have been trying to make him call George, but he is one of those stones that requires to be broken apart to be able to turn it around." Suspicion was the last thing they expected from Tinashe; they were playing him like a pawn in a chess game. On the phone, they kept on exchanging ideas and challenges, also real obstacles currently occurring during the absence of communication.

These men had formed a mutual business relationship, all brought together to face one enemy. After three minutes on the phone, the call dropped.

AFTER HAVING BEEN IGNORED FOR few minutes, Joey went on to seek more attention for himself. "I hope we can depend on him to be effective and efficient."

"Such high expectations usually bring a bad result," Foster replied. He believed that Jadea could pull this off, but he was surely starting to doubt, following the negative comments from Joey.

Jadea started his engine again, driving his car back into the road. He had failed to give Tinashe a proper reason to call. The next thing was to force him so that he could penetrate George's heart. Jadea had made a promise never to hurt the boy in any situation, so he remained soft and easy on him. They wanted George on a silver platter. Jadea had no idea who he was about to face on the battleground: a man who had killed more than once. Tinashe had wanted his father for a very long time, but this was not the father he had hoped for.

"Jadea is holding the boy. You said so. Then we should bring him into the police station for security reasons." Foster and Joey were facing each other. Joey's mentality towards criminals by name and the society was always raw. It was wrong and he had forgotten one thing and that is that a criminal mind was as bad-mannered as any other.

He kept on repeating the same question: would Jadea get it done? These questions were starting to annoy Foster, which was the purpose and Joey's particular talent. Foster never stopped protecting Jadea in their eyes. "Yeah, I am quite sure. It is any easy one." His phone vibrated in his pocket. "Jadea is calling."

George's picture kept on flowing in the back of his mind: saved information in the back of his head. Portraying him as Dad was another thing. He finished smoking a cigarette and threw it away. He thought about making that call. Emotions can be a burden if coming from a point of pain and they had struck his face again. The juice between them could not blend enough to make a sweet serenade – there was no way to hide that. It was not a wall between them but rather a bridge, hidden by overflowing water not in the right season.

"WHY SHOULD I CARE? THIS is a killer and to him I am currently dead." Tinashe needed no father and when he gained confidence again he was sure of it. Whatever Jadea wanted to pull off, he was going to be pulled out of it. He was also a dead man, if he could not be discreet enough. Furthermore, everybody gets a second chance after ruining the first one. His involvement in this started making him realise there was a lot at stake, and a high probability of getting himself killed by a third party. If he were to be quick enough if anything were to go wrong, he had to find himself a second plan. "*Whenever there is Plan A, a person gets an extra twenty-five second chance. You should plan until up to plan Z to get your things in order.*" He thought to himself of how to sort this out. His way out could be smoothed when it was time. He had been playing these games for a long time; it went back to what he had always been doing to earn his living. After the darkest night always comes a brighter morning: remember that!

Tinashe's light at the end of the tunnel had always been his friends. They understood him as well as he understood them, although he had never considered it that way until now. Car wash and security of parked cars was his normal job and that was as far as he could go without selling weed, or anything related, or the more dangerous crack.

They were now drinking energized drinks, Tinashe leaning his back against the car. It were as if they were waiting for someone, but horror was in their thoughts against each other. They were caught up in a moment, listening to the radio loudly enough that a person a few metres away could know which radio station it was, if they were only familiar with it. Jadea held a cigarette in his other hand, Tinashe was craving for another one again, but his idea that cigarettes would take away his issues was idle. Sometimes, he would walk around looking for stubs just to finish them up, but this day was his lucky day.

They continued making jokes and laughing. He felt free around Jadea to the point that he asked for the whole box of cigarettes after one skiff and went from a cigarette to a pack without hesitation. Jadea took a pack from the dashboard and gave it to Tinashe. He knew this was to level up the tension between them. The cigarettes regulated his stress level, clearing his mind to open a new page, but his lungs would bear the brunt of the cancer that would be the long-term effect.

Both of them were away from their troubles of life. Hypocrisies, in-between smiles and crocodile tears, flowed like the Kariba Dam. They waited for what was to come. They'd had both had guns held against their faces, and knew about fear.

Chapter 4

George was sitting in his old Grand Cherokee. He put in the key and the engine started running bit by bit; then he turned it off again, removed the keys and threw them on the dashboard, while his brain had thoughts circulating faster than the blood circulating in his veins. This was a new belief that surely Tinashe was his son, lost in the wilderness, whom he had almost killed. And at the same time he was happy that the boy was not dead.

He wished to see him again and really look into his eyes to see if he could see himself in him, but already there were similarities in their characters. He knew that the boy was the last thing to perfect his life, for he had money already. Trying to remember the boy's name was only giving him more headaches. He could see how ignorant he had been; there was no need to look in the mirror for a different answer.

Firstly he was a father and then he'd gone on to become a holder of the key of life. If he wished for somebody to die, it would happen.

Looking up at an eighty-degree angle, stretching his hands out, he reminisced: "*That time in a deep, illegal mining shaft, unable to support myself after two bullets damaged me, the one hit the thigh and the other only damaged the rib. The pain I felt that day changed me forever.*"

A pain that comes from the heart is harder than physical pain, because physical pain you can ease up with medication but the one of betrayal has no medicine other than forgiveness.

Thinking back on how they had robbed him and left him to die – his so-called friends – hurt him. It had made him a very angry person since then. Now he had found new peace: a son. He had never been there to see him growing up and to teach him anything with absolute certainty like his father before him.

When he had been imprisoned for six years in a four-man cell he had thought about having his own family. He'd once had a wife and they'd tried to have a child many times but had failed. It had made his wife angry against those other woman aborting a blessing because of their unorganised sexual life, while she was never given the chance to have her own.

Likewise, George had taught himself to be positive all the time and he was full of limitless confidence. He believed no man was bigger. He kept saying that things were going to work out. These were old chances that life was throwing back at him again; the same chances he had once reflected.

He had been born a warrior; already he had planned to give them a century of cows if they wanted beef. Revenge and war take two graves to end it: a fifty-fifty probability, win or lose. A friend in prison had once told him: *Do not anticipate problems for if you do you will never go forward in life. You will become a recluse, and go into a shell. That is why there are many followers and few leaders in this world. You have to be the one to take chances and later you are going to be well, make the sacrifice. You get knocked down once, you get up again. You get knocked down twice, you get up until you come to a third time when you come to cross those roads and it becomes history. Either you disintegrate or you say, "It is just another time," and keep on going forward.*

The more you have lost, the more you will be knocked down and have to bounce back. Treat a man like a dog and literally he becomes a dog, but the trick is not to become what they want you to become. You've got to keep your dignity and your pride.

George had stepped out of his car to think freely. The weather was cloudy and windy, such a perfect day and not as tiring as it could be when it was very hot. He was left with a choice to take what he had and leave, but that was like letting your crops be savaged by worms. In one way he was disadvantaged, but it was also a two way leverage. He'd made sure of that. No matter what choices he was left to make, it was anyway a suicidal mission either way.

He stepped back into the vehicle and closed the door. He grabbed the keys he had left on the dashboard. His eyes red like a chicken liver, he picked up his speed so much that the car was near its limit.

TINASHE STARTED THINKING ABOUT LEAVING Jadea and wondered what the chance was since he was in an open area. Finishing up one of the many cigarettes he had smoked, he thought, *"If I do not take care of myself, nobody will"*. It was a bold and pregnant idea. He would rather take a chance than stick around with people who were using him big time.

Changing his life forever could be by starting up a new relationship with the father he'd never had before, or going back to the streets and the old life of bags, hustling out weed and crack, where life was more about his stomach than anything else. Although not many people knew this, he had a very different interest in art, which was an unrealised talent and a dream. *"Dreams are nightmares because they will never come true,"* his friend would say.

Intentions and attentions had turned his mood around. He was just learning how to use a touch screen phone properly. He'd never owned one. He only knew about it from other people, even though these days it had turned into a need and a part of life. He kept on dialling the number until he got it right. He did not press the green button in the corner, and placed the phone on top of the car.

Some young college girls who were passing by had caught Jadea's attention and he wanted them to notice him. Whatever was going through Tinashe's mind at that moment was none of his business. He was sure they were together, steadily careless. The girls were already keeping him busy. He'd crushed marijuana and mixed it with cigarette tobacco, so they were probably getting high.

Tinashe had had enough of it. He cancelled all the digits that were on the screen. Nervous and paranoid feelings had him.

Jadea was a distance away from Tinashe, talking to the girls, and when he looked for Tinashe, the young man was nowhere to be found. He was already far away, lifting one foot after the other and running for his life. Jadea was left startled like never before. He left the girls in a hurry, running towards his car. Like everyone else, he had underestimated the young boy.

He wanted to pull out a Magnum, but the girls had followed to the car again. Surprisingly, they thought they had just run into a so called *blesser*, the new way to earn income nowadays for young females, so they kept on staring at him. A Magnum was going to attract unnecessary attention. The park had few people but enough to notice a gun when they saw one. He took action. He grabbed the car keys out of his pocket. It was not funny anymore.

He realised that even his phone was gone too. The more Tinashe spent time with them, the more educated he became about the other side of life, the side he'd always wanted. And there was Jadea, confused in the middle of people who seemed to care only about their own business – their social life in particular – and always in contact with online friends. He thought they were missing the point of life. Time is money but never can money be time. Money lost could be recovered but time lost is forever irrecoverable.

Jadea kept his eyes on the rear-view mirror, one hand on the steering wheel and the other on the gear stick. He kept his long legs on the accelerator. "*The curse of working with kids!*" His mind was full of this frustration. It seemed as if he had consumed a catalyst to speed up his reactions, which were close to being involuntary.

He drove at a speed that suggested that he had stolen the car. Fear for his life was part of his aggressive driving. Fraternizing with the enemy does not always work as expected. He'd survived using harsh ways of life, with all the ambitions he had that came from his father who'd had more love for alcohol than love for his son. He had been forced to grow up in the hands of survivors.

As he droved down the streets, Jadea kept his eyes everywhere until he realised he needed more eyes at every corner. Meanwhile, Tinashe saw the opportunity of a car going into a garage and decided to join it before an electric gate closed. Two black security guards saw him coming in. They were in blue uniforms and they wore caps. They noticed him because the right procedure to use when coming in the garage entrance on foot was to use the inside door, not the exit one.

"Hey, Champ," Tinashe said. They were bored and relaxed, opening the garage gate up and down to the usual tenants. Tinashe changed their mood and when he'd calmed himself down so that they too could be calm, it was like he'd meant to make the visit. He built self-confidence before being chased away. He started the conversation first because going back out there would be hell now. The garage had closed. He'd worked out a small plan as he was approaching them. He had the phone that belonged to Jadea. Only faith in God kept everything in perfect shape, as if it were planned.

"I am here to see Dumelatswa," he lied them.

"Who?" one of the guards replied because they were not familiar with this name.

"The name again?" the other security officer asked in a local dialect. Tinashe said, "I am here to see him. He wants to buy my phone. Dumelatswa."

"Which phone?" Curiously, they wanted to be involved with whatever this Dumelatswa wanted from this young man; it was simple psychology. The conversation had began flowing. "Let me see the phone first." They walked along to a small security office, where a guard was sitting down, helping a tenant's friend to sign in.

He took out the phone that belonged to Jadea and actually entered the security code correctly. In their eyes, this made it obvious that it belonged to him. He gave the guard the phone, who was quick to smile. He wanted it.

"How much is it?" He had seen something to show off to his friends, and he looked at the young man and thought he could take chances to manipulate the price to suit his needs. That is how the governing system worked nowadays. As much as he wanted it, he looked upon it as just an easy deal with an amateur, who was obviously a drug addict from his looks.

Confusing a sheep with a wolf had Jadea sweating, as if he had run a ten-kilometre marathon. Looking over his shoulder angrily, he wanted to kill Tinashe at that moment. Unfortunately, there was no miracle for him. He knew that God was not there whenever he called out for changes. His unconscious mind caused all the ignorance and arrogance that was ruining his life. *If I am not given it, then I can take it by force*. He was dedicated enough to pursue what he wanted, perhaps until he was somewhere in a graveyard.

He carried too much pride to call Foster and tell him that something had gone sour, so he let the thought go. It was anyway too early; only twenty minutes had passed. He had slowed the speed down, and now two hands carefully held the steering wheel with a firm grip. His big eyes could not see anything that appeared to be familiar or would indicate Tinashe's trail. Only a devil in him had taken over. Anger issues had trapped him and he went to the nearest liquor store to buy a small bottle of spirits.

His search lasted him one and a half hours before he started seeking new ways to deal with this. He knew that the more he delayed alerting someone who knew the boy better, the harder it was going to be to find him. Firstly, he went to the cell phone dealers nearby to get himself a new phone in order to call his own phone. Then he was going to acquire more guys to help him out by using their resources. They were people who owed him favours.

Foster had a little experience with George because of what he had gone through. As long his shoulder was still in pain, he was reminded of what had happened. It was clear that Jadea's irresponsibility was going to fall on Foster's shoulders and he would be held accountable for losing control over their moneybags. Joey and Detective Mduduzi played different roles in this. The detective had paved the way for this deal to happen, just to make some extra, while Joey was in charge of transfers, but this was a chance for them to make new lives out of this stone dealing thing. They were both in terror as their hands were still empty at this time. The information that George had found in that bag included a collective number of customer names.

Jadea was given the right directions to reach a dealer's place. He spent time talking to the sellers, asking questions about whether a phone could be traced with immediate effect. He'd thought nobody in their right mind would ever touch what belonged to him, which meant that the tracker was never on. He took some money out of his pocket and exchanged it for a phone from the man who was behind the counter. The man behind the counter took the battery out of the plastic, placed it into the phone and covered it. It was on now and working properly, but still he had one problem: that was the contacts in the other phone. Without any option, he went back into the car to go through to the police station. Another problem he had to deal with.

Tinashe was not startled by the few bucks that the security officers gave him for the phone. It was enough for him to lay low until things had calmed down. For the time being, his feelings did not matter, as long as his pocket was full enough for his stomach. The cell phone had paved the way for him.

Coming out of the garage, the gate half opened. As he left, he clearly painted a picture in his head of a father who was insanely sick. In his heart, he had no one to trust, although he wished to. His thoughtful plans made his ways as unique as that of an artist. He stood outside with the roller-gate behind him closing slowly. The phone he'd got on top of the money from the security guard was in his pocket without a sim card. It didn't matter to him. A thought crossed his mind about buying drugs first, before escaping into another town to start another life. He felt he had nothing to lose. Meth rang the bells in his thoughts; he was totally addicted to it.

He looked around the main roads just for his safety, but it felt like he was the only one walking in the road. He watched out for a suspicious car or movement, any signs of Jadea's goons. He was convinced that he had won the first round.

"Now for sure I have something to show up with to my broke friends," he thought. New clothes and a few bucks was enough for him to give gratitude and appreciate what the day had given him. If days were bad for him and his friend Makhathini, they borrowed a trolley just to collect empty plastic bottles. If there was nothing else to do, the only way to get something fresh to eat was to dig it out the bins that the restaurants constantly used or pick up fruit that the street vendors had left behind.

He walked down a street looking at people, small business shops and small supermarkets. Pedestrians increased as he approached the heart of a central business district. Private car drivers and taxi drivers could not stop shouting at each other to give way. Other taxis along the road picked up people waiting to go to different destinations, and those who had their private cars parked along the side road were having arguments, refusing parking tickets.

Tinashe crossed that road to another block. They had known him there for more than a year, usually from buying something to get himself high with. Most pushers sat with a small table scattered with different cigarettes, sweets and snacks.

Friendly Tinashe was a usual customer of the place, but his conversation with them was obviously short. They called him "boi-boi". He took the money out of his pocket and gave it to them.

This was a simple transaction of buying drugs: no formalities and questions asked, as long you knew what you came for.

He waited for the hustler to come back, as drugs were hidden elsewhere. At last he came back with a folded black plastic and gave it to Tinashe, who forced it into his pocket.

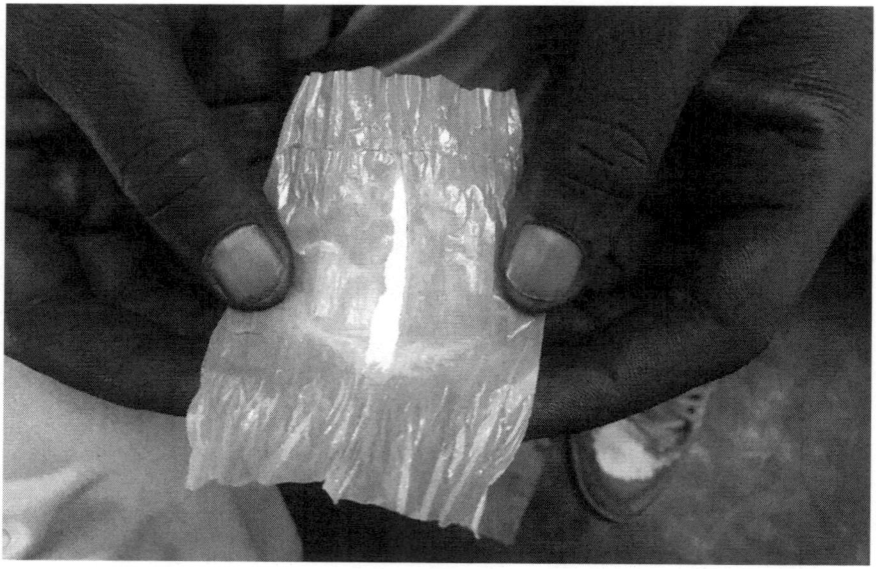

Chapter 5

George thought and wondered about it repeatedly. Tinashe had reincarnated and he was sure it sounded like a story he had once been told. A perfect destiny, that was all it is and shall be.

What he had in the stolen bags was a perfect retirement plan for George, and he knew better than most that these chances are not usual. This plan had taken him six years behind bars to be able to pull it off, and he had promised himself that he was never going to be locked again in that cage. He had fortune enough to disappear forever. Apart from avoiding jail, his concern now was to make a call to Joey and Detective Mduduzi for arrangements in return for his son. All thoughts that conceptualised in his head were absolutely perfect but seconds were turning into minutes, minutes into hours and hours into days and it made him nervous. He felt like the one who was running out of time before a whole mob was sent after him like a pack of dogs.

He dialled the number to the office. Before making that call, he had texted someone and that person seemed to know all about these things because he kept encouraging George from the beginning. His thoughts became more clear and his mind more conscious and enlightened.

They usually say that a man coming out of the correctional system is worse than when he went in. At first this was true for George – "undemocratic thuggery" were the words that his parole officer had used and that defined him a lot. However, he quickly changed after receiving the news about Tinashe.

BY THE TIME JADEA REACHED the Central Private Investigation Group (CPIG), Tinashe was kicking it back in a hustling spot. The only alternative was to hide until evening. He stared at his old-life pair of shoes, blanket and some unnecessary things he'd picked up. After collecting all into a refuse bag – where it belonged in the first place – and considering that all the property he'd ever owned could fit into one refuse bag and still leave space for more things, he tied it tight.

He went to a bin close by and left his once-owned possessions inside it. His faith and eagerness to change the way he was living were undefined. He destroyed his demons after realising that once you survive you realise that death and life have been obstacles holding you back. Get rich or die trying. Money thoughts made him at least know who he could be in the following days or months or years: if he just traced the money, searching for his birth right. "Where is my father?" The little information he had from Jadea was enough to start digging.

Tinashe opened the plastic from a dealer and took two packages out of it. What remained he put back into his pocket.

HESITATION AFTER MAKING UP YOUR mind is a temptation. George closed his eyes and leaned against the car seat, gripping the steering wheel and meditating about *money and family.*

He knew that in the search, to have it all you might have to lose it all first. That was the sacrifice that gave him only seconds. He knew that such men were capable of wiping him off the face of the earth for profit. Open your ears in real silence and you could hear hell screaming when your soul is gone and all you wish is to have it back.

He made a call to someone to give him the information he needed for his next move, before his emotions took decisions for him. He knew that just missing one piece of it could mean that his head and body could be two hundred kilometres apart the next morning.

"What's up? Do you remember JM? I came to see you a long time back with him."

The person on the phone replied, “Yeah, I do remember him. Shorter than me and white!” he exclaimed.

George added, “I have something that is precious to him, and he was sent to take it away from me, and he is going crazy for it. Nevertheless, he claims to be holding something of value to me, that is leverage. I want extra ears and hands. I need your crew.”

He dialled the gentleman, who picked up quickly. If it was more quickly than necessary, it was a sign of desperate times, bad for such businesses and strongly not suggested as its proves weakness. When you think about being hard, then you stick to it with a gun under your pillow every day and one eye open all the time. After this conversation, some did not ever come back home for dinner.

THEY PICKED UP THE CALL. “Have you made up your mind now,” said Joey. George, for a second, was silent. Raising his voice he replied, “Rand Club, twelve noon,” and then he cut the call. He was not open for any other conversation.

Joey was from the yards and in love with his long time wife. He was referred to as a sergeant with a penchant for complaining. Whenever he was in a conversation with someone about a business idea, he would argue to the point of threatening whoever was a problem – and one thing about his threats was that they were usually accompanied by action. He never let down his ego.

GEORGE HAD CUT THE CALL and started calling one of his loyal friends who had actually protected him while he was inside the prison. The favours between them were many. He was in need of another favour and before the call he texted someone by the name of Cooper. Whoever this person was, he was important to him. He kept him in the loop.

His conscience accused him as a father who’d lost time to see his son grow and the thought took him on a journey of his whole life in the blink of an eye.

This is what the judge once asked him before sentence: "Tell about your whole life to this day?"

"We were raised in rural areas. My grandfather relocated there during the time of colonisation and my father was still young during the period. My father's heritage from his father was the land that he grew up farming, finding whatever he could produce out of his garden to feed his family. It was an area that was affected by war for freedom. My older brother joined the struggle and never came back home again, and it depressed my mother when she was called to identify his body. As I was growing, many things changed; the influence for the struggle was everywhere. When I was old enough to move out of my father's home, I moved into the townships. We started by having simple jobs in the CBD just to keep us going to see the next day. My father always kept on encouraging us about going to school and finding success out of it, and the heart wanted it but the pockets did not go along. Some young people like us, from nowhere, were making successful stories getting richer and that made me start writing my own destination at the age twenty-four. Our minds were living large."

In the office, Foster remained calm and seated as Joey furiously had his hands on Jadea's neck, pressing him tightly into a corner, after a long argument and finger pointing about Jadea's defensive opinions, which bothered Joey Morish. He made a fool out of himself but the people around understood the reasons behind this act. Detective Mduduzi stood up from his chair to calm him down.

Foster did not do anything but remain seated. He had enough problems to deal with. Joey took his hands off Jadea after Foster had looked at him steadily for about ten seconds. He was angry with him, it seemed. Then Jadea walked out. This was not him getting off the hook but simply meant he was going to find a solution. They wanted answers within one hour.

Joey was like a mad dog because of his obsession with killing George and it was too much for him to bear, too much pressure because of their unfinished business.

It was not a time for jokes, so everybody remained quiet after Jadea walked out, although the detective thought, "*This was stupid of Joey. We still wanted the boy from him. He is making this all harder, bit by bit.*"

George did not have a proper place to rest his head. The time he had spent in his car was that of an anxious person, without anywhere to go. Probably he did not have a proper plan but this had not been necessary until he received a news leak text:

"HE IS NOT IN THE POLICE STATION.
NONE OF THEM KNOWS WHERE HE IS
AND HE IS NOT DEAD. MAKE A PLAN"

With nowhere to run, he drove his car to go to look for Tinashe. He did not know where to start his search, and the pressure was not relieved, but the venture was different.

The dark was falling on top of Mduduzi's head. An ice cream truck was slowly moving out on the road, making much noise and irritating the three gentlemen who sat together to seek a solution on how to capture George easily. It was hopeless having him and torturing him to give them the diamonds that were smuggled out of Zimbabwe through the borders illegally. These countries remained either war-torn or economy-torn apparently. Even after killings, torture and outrageous human rights abuses in Zimbabwe's diamond industry, Zimbabwe has been welcomed into the community of diamond producing nations.

In 2008, the Zimbabwean army seized the valuable Marange diamond deposit in eastern Zimbabwe, massacring more than two hundred diamond miners who stood in the way. Soldiers then enslaved local adults and children in the diamond fields, beating and torturing those who disobeyed. An estimated two billion dollars in diamond wealth disappeared, mostly into the hands of military leaders. The army then put private companies in charge of mining.

However, community members are still being beaten and killed, relocated families live in poverty, corruption continues, and nobody has been held accountable for past crimes. At no point did the news publishers print the story. It had many powerful people to expose, and they could not play around with it.

Joey and Foster walked out of the office, leaving Detective Mduduzi behind. The station head had sniffed something off with his detective after he'd seen his long time friend, Joey. Now the plate under the pass was hot. The Colonel realised that this crime was different from all other normal city robberies, and he called those who were familiar with the crime that Petrus and Joey were working on.

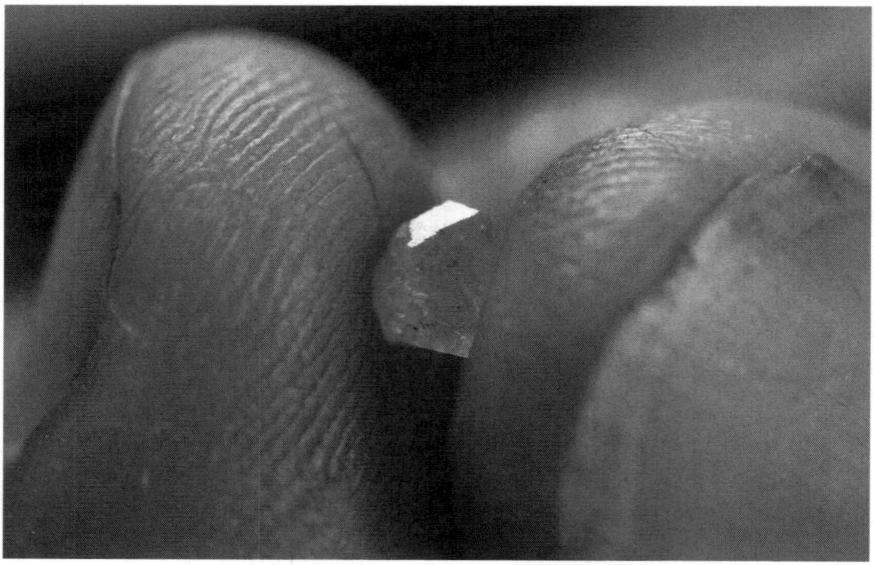

Confrontation 1
Detective versus the Colonel

"Good morning." At about 11h30 their conversation had begun. "Why are these guys sticking around here like paper glue, and we are attracting flies all over this place."

Petrus closed the door. Hearing unfavourable words coming from his boss' mouth, he smiled to ease up the tension. It always worked with him.

"Good morning, Sir." The Colonel had had enough of it. His name and department were being dragged through unnecessary mud and it always comes with its consequences, not to mention the press.

"Explain yourself? Joey boy is trouble wherever he goes. It is not good for our place right now, after all the work we have accomplished in the last months. What is he still doing here? The truth is that George has come back into your lives, and this time heavily!" he exclaimed.

Detective Mduduzi replied, "We are supposed to be meeting up with him in fifteen minutes. In exchange we promised him his son but we lost contact with the boy about two hours ago. We are not worried about the amount he is holding, but our concern is something very valuable to all these organisations and a powerful individual: a list that George has that includes the names of high profile customers such as retired ministers and others of such status.

"A man with one part of his heart held back by grievances. he is likely to causes pain if his hands are holding power. George's actions are motivated by what happened to him. He feels deeply betrayed and he is going to take many of these bastards down personally. Unfortunately, he has enough strength to do it and the timing as well."

The Colonel was flabbergasted. "So how can I be of help to defuse the situation faster?" This situation had come as a surprise and was dangerous. It could cause an enormous and very threatening war if it leaked. He calculated the mathematics, which proved how hard it was.

Detective Mduduzi knew that at least he had back up. He was told to switch off the blue lights. He knew all the excesses to handle it, including the power of authority.

Confrontation 2
Joey versus Unknown Agent

"Where are we, Sergeant, can you update me?" This was a male wearing a leather jacket like the one Joey had worn the previous day, but this person was bald headed.

"I have nothing to update. I just got on this case a few hours ago, and you cannot be seriously asking that."

"Is that so?" the man replied.

"Okay. Get this sorted out quickly or the contract is given to someone else. We thought you could handle it better since this was on your plate and your mess."

"Twenty-four hours," Joey said, putting all his files back into the briefcase. Time was speeding up so much for him that he could not stop thinking about it. He could not back down on his plan either, but would rather take his chances going forward with it, and fifteen minutes to twelve noon was the time on his watch.

Confrontation 3
Foster versus Jadea

FOSTER FOLLOWED JADEA TO TALK to him.

"They wanted to cut you off, but since you were the last one in contact with the boy the blues have to be involved to track him fast."

Foster was talking to Jadea about how he also felt sorry about what had happened to him, but surely Jadea was responsible. After all, he'd promised to kept it real but cocaine and his addiction to marijuana was like that of a religious Rastafari.

They'd decided to have the conversation away from the police station. They never felt safe being inside. They were both from one of the most disastrous streets of southern Africa. They were able to talk about it, and it was Foster who convinced Jadea to come back to the office. He put his feelings aside; they were just in a rough business. He gave Jadea the example of what had happened to his shoulder, and they drove back to the station.

THEY OPENED THE DOOR AFTER knocking and heard a "Come in".

The belly of beast of 28s and 26s had come across. "How is your arm, Foster?" They had been expecting the detective but someone else was there: the person who'd supplied connections to Foster since day one. He was one of the flies that had been attracted just to cause more confusion in the middle of a war. After hearing big numbers were playing, he was tempted. They had not expected to see his face so soon.

"Relax." He offered them a seat and poured water into three glasses laid on the table. They sat firmly and each picked up a glass of water. Already their lives were dried up by a business that had drained their blood and energy, not to mention thoughts.

"Jadea, a rumour has it that you messed up again."

"Silly joke," Jadea replied but truly he was not just disappointed but embarrassed also. Such a child had made a fool out of him.

Then, this man said to Jadea "Do not worry about it. It will pass at the end of the day."

"Cut the long story short. What do you want?" asked Jadea angrily. He smelt a rat and a snake close by. Nobody has a good heart when it comes to politics and money. It is about how much control you seek and it is endless games with those whose eyes are on the fortune. People have played the same game for thousands of years.

"As I said, relax. I do not want to be a part of this. I have a lot to lose anyway. I just came to wish you well over the coming days because you might start burying each other. Keep your heads up."

It was a quick conversation and he was just someone passing by.

Jadea and Foster remained seated. Detective Mduduzi and Joey walked in one after the other. A few minutes later a phone rang. The caller ID made them shake but they were now sure that no matter how much they did not have any of the bags or the information, George was not going anywhere anymore. Now he was calling shots and none of them wanted to answer the phone, although they strongly desired to hear whatever George had to say.

Detective Mduduzi Mduduzi picked up the call.

"Hello, George," he replied.

"Before I show up, stop playing mind tricks and put the boy on the phone." George told them the one thing they were all expecting but they deeply hated hearing it out loud and clear, which they could do as Petrus had stuck his finger on the loudspeaker button. No stunt could be pulled from this one.

"We locked him away. You deliver and we deliver," he lied.

George's voice became deeper and colder. "This is a joke," and he repeated the same question.

Detective Mduduzi started saying many words, negotiating, but they were for street thugs, not this type. He was sure they'd lost him and indeed, George dropped the call and it was untraceable.

Joey could not stop cursing. They all stood up to go and look for the boy before George got to him first. Petrus had also not heard anything from the search party he had sent into the streets. Loose ends were everywhere. However, he went to double check with the team. His assistant officer told him they did not have anything yet of help, but he did hand him an envelope.

"WHEN YOU SAY LIVING LARGE, what do you mean by that?" The judge knew exactly what he asked in the court room. Out of interest he wanted to know George's different version of struggle.

"Whatever we had in our hands, we would sell to avoid danger and suspicious police or to whoever knew about what it was. That made us blow money in clubs and other expensive places. The black market was easy to find, if your buyers were loyal to you. We were young, dumb and stupid when we were introduced to illegal mining, because this was just the beginning of it in Africa, after the white regimes had taken these mines and manipulated the markets for themselves. We found loopholes. Many politicians and legit businessman were educated but broke. They wanted some sort of capital for their campaigns and new companies. We got involved and became their guys in exchange for favours. By the end of that same year, we were supporting regime change and it worked. We knew nothing except the stones we carried around. They gave us power to be the untouchable all over southern Africa and that impact forced us to remain unknown to the outside world.

"We had new cars and new friends, which however was not so good at the end of it. Some friend I had…" He stopped talking to think for a moment, and then he continued, "…they wanted my connections only and to know how my things were working out so fast. In such a business you are alone, and around snakes that hiss in your face, ears, home, and everywhere. Jealous for power and money, they started causing all the inconveniences, and then people started dying one by one.

"Those whom we once sponsored, especially politicians after they had won and got into power, thought we had long tails, so they were cutting loose ends to protect their secrets. We had a series of events that we survived by luck and it was deepening inside of us, creating roots of protecting shields.

"Because I had those things that I was taught to pursue in life, I got married at twenty-six to my first wife and I told myself I had it all. For sure, money was not a problem by then, but my character and behaviour as a married man did not qualify for Angela. I was still not satisfied, either in my house or outside of it. Soon, I was out with my other ordinary friends. We'd get drunk and I would still play around with other females. It got so bad that my own wife was no longer on my time line story. Other friends of mine showed me how to play well.

"I went on to think I had some kind of a burden, to the point that I went to seek advice from *sangomas* and spiritual leaders to point out right from wrong, and wrongs from right. That was more burden to me.

"I went back to introduce my wife to my father but he warned me I was too young to be married. I told him that he did not understand any of this and he was too old school. Later on, after two years, I lost my father to cancer. Angela was one of a kind and a beauty that is incomparable."

George's life seemed organised but it had a disorder. It was properly planned and the fast lane was all he knew. He tried having a child but failed so many times that he sought comfort in alcohol. Only his wife knew that, and such things always change a man for the worse. If he carries no faith in him, it becomes the worst of him.

They were friends with Joey already, a white boy. Joey also had a nephew who was always around him. Later, he was killed and since then their relationship had been strained. They were still close but deep down Joey blamed George for his nephew's death. There was a great conspiracy about the death. A backstabber of them all, Joey did not have one enemy but many and few of them respected Joey.

They crossed borders and ran into a police officer who knew more about them than they thought. As long money was going into his pocket, he decided to protect their interests. When they were arrested over an allegation, they would not even reach the police station: who dared cuff the donors? Young officers too were introduced to the benefit of being an officer of the law and one of those officers at the time was Petrus who had a very close relationship with the senior officer. Police protect corruption and criminals when they are making a living out of it.

Politics and politicians, even to this day, have hidden agendas every time. Their money circulates between them in brown envelopes, passed around from one hand to another. The foolishness of individuals of power is that they become comfortable in their positions above the law; they get used to it and have a tendency to take it for granted. Leaders should never become masters of the law, but servants of it.

Joey's nephew had conspired against everyone, troublesome child. Joey had security friends in the mines. The team would go in and out of the mines at any time of the day and at any moment. The business was going well throughout and they achieved many accomplishments. Then a problem arose when George thought of himself as being in the same position that Joey was in, and stopped depending on him for links. The relationship was starting to be hectic, and he wanted to be alone and independent. Josh, the nephew, had already warned Joey that this might happen.

Naturally, two Alphas cannot survive in one pack. George was twenty-nine by that time, but his loyalty to the crew was still real. All he wanted was to cut the ties without blood, but in this hustle that is not possible. They make you feel like you have a blood bond. You cannot quit or change loyalty. Just like African dictatorships, organised crime requires your body and soul.

It was a conflict of business. Other diamond poachers were murdered all the time just to get the stones off them. Angola had refused to acknowledge these problems. Instead, it filed criminal defamation charges against a journalist who documented more than a hundred murders and the torture of more than five hundred people in two diamond mining towns. Soldiers routinely demanded bribes, beating and killing miners who did not cooperate. And a flourishing diamond trade has not made Angola a more responsible diamond producer. Angola's diamond fields are once again the scene of horrific violence. They have also been rounding up tens of thousands of migrants each year and expelling them across the border, raping many of the women first.

George and Joey shared equally and never again dared to speak a word about it. They knew they were destined for hell. They had nothing more to lose but making more money. George become the gatekeeper, he fought his way to it.

He and Angela tried to have some time set aside just for them, but George kept on failing her until she took advice from her friends and sisters that it was truly a failed marriage. She could sense the tension hurting her too. Their sexual relationship was poor. She got to the point where she could not see herself when she looked into the mirror. After a very long time, she had arguments over simple things and the only thing they surely agreed on was to be divorced and that was easier than expected. Angela's family had it all, so she went home in one peace instead of pieces, unlike what happened in other marriages. They'd handled it as the elders.

Six months after his first marriage had broken up, George had another wife for himself. The argument that had ravaged his previous marriage was about his job, about which he had not been specific. But he was introduced to his second wife through a friend, as successful as he was. Nothing mattered but being worshipped and praised. He could provide for her, and that was her only concern. The reality was she was in for money only and without it she would have walked out to another donor. Financial freedom was what she was always after, and she was of extraordinary beauty so that no man around her could deny her temptations: an ebony queen.

Since he'd moved from the townships to the suburbs and had become the city owner, he had young followers everywhere, ready to take his order at any time. He was a well-established gangster in their eyes. He urbanized their spirits and fertilised a seed, like a sperm in a womb, in their heads. He became powerful enough to control others, so he had many enemies. When it came to his job, he lifted his head way, way up. From a rural boy to a city king, a little story matured into a bigger one. He acted like an upright person in the public but privately he was something else.

He spent a lot of time on himself and he actually thought of himself as a peaceful role model. He only remembered his friends who never saw it to the end, but were wiped off the face of the earth at young ages. He never lost his focus, and he was determined to get more and more stones even though the world had its own frustrations and depressions. Many families had lost relatives to HIV and AIDS. The topic was as viral as funerals; it was at its peak point.

Furthermore, he had many young women around him. To this day in southern Africa, the girls between *sixteen and twenty-five* experience the highest incidence of HIV and AIDS, not to mention other sexually transmitted diseases such as syphilis, which they are getting from different age groups, including rich men way older than them. After they are infected, they bring these diseases to the young males, eager to have sex.

George could not find the perfect satisfaction for his lust needs. He believed that one of the girls he'd had while he was getting around had got pregnant and had borne him Tinashe, although he was uncertain about this.

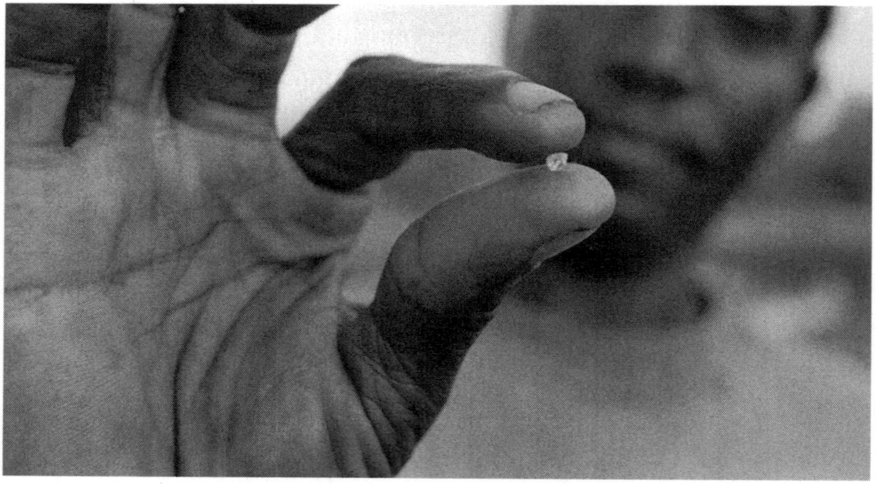

Chapter 6

Tinashe's friends came close to him, as if he held salvation in his hands. Surely, Nyaope is heaven to these kids in their eyes, but literally speaking they are living in hell. They just want to be left alone.

Jadea in the meantime had promised himself not to let pressure get to him. He'd just had too much for that morning. Tinashe at his age could not share with anyone what had happened the previous day: seeing a man bleeding, lying on the pavement dying; walking over just to get the bags that were in the car. Jadea had miscalculated him, but things such as this always leave a man changed. Give a thought to the kids in mid-east and other African countries with wars that cannot lay to rest, being born in a war zone. The only chance and education they can get is about military warfare. Those two shots that left a security guard bleeding made him look into the man's eyes. They both wanted to say something but they had met in a critical situation.

When Tinashe met Foster, whether he was a pawn or not, it was a life-changing moment for him. He'd told Foster a few weeks back that he had given himself a purpose. He felt awakened. Everything seemed to be easier after just a few words of motivation. He watched closely as weeks passed by, realising that a delivery boy could read between the lines.

Around his friends, he had a different attitude, one that was free and happy at all times. They had one thing in common, which was that they had nothing in life. After smoking weed, they could joke and laugh for entertainment. Before they smoked marijuana, they would mix it with Nyaope, that well-known rat poison, the consumption of which destroys the whole body. After that, if it was a lucky day such as this one, they would follow it with crystal methamphetamine, aka crack or tik, a legal compound under the brand name Desoxyn which is infrequently prescribed to treat obesity, narcolepsy and attention deficit hyperactivity disorder. Cracking jokes until it is late and addictions will turn you into someone who cares about nothing else.

The *Chill Spot*, they had come to call it; an enclosed space without wind and they usually used a toilet as a smoking area. One pulled out a glass tube with an open hole, a cylindrically shaped chamber to liquefy solid into gas; then they would pull the gas from the other hole. A good pull is called a *scout*, which means consuming quantities in one pull that might be a real danger, even to the point of instant death. If it goes into the wrong pipe then you choke and cough.

They had used a lighter to heat it from solid form, melting it until it turned to gas.

Tinashe held the lighter on, and his friend had the pipe in his mouth. "Wait, let me do it for you." The chemical slowly got into the lungs. After a long pull, they let it out. His friends, Makhathini and Sandi, had become professionals at this. After every smoke there was a sudden stop to check how much was left. They would feel as if their spirits had been lifted up so high. A drug makes itself a comfortable tool and a daily activity to its consumer.

From nowhere, one of his friends who smoked meth came running after him; he'd known exactly where to find them. He was sweating and banged the door from the outside as it was locked from the inside. Paranoid and nervous again, Tinashe dropped the tube out of fear. He had forgotten his problems and he was about to be reminded of them again. The tube broke. They opened the door, as the friend shouted to them from outside. Tinashe choked from the disturbing noise, which is one of the most important things to avoid when consuming crystal. He coughed and breathed deeply.

"There is a man looking for you outside."

He stopped to listen to this important message. "What man?" he asked, although he knew exactly who was out there.

"Police, like." He caught a breath again, and their eyes met. He thought, "*Maybe I could tell them about this,*" but he decided against it. Anything is possible with street life.

He stood up straight and wondered if it was Jadea. The others were not as eager to find him as Jadea was, so he was sure it might be him.

"Where is he?" he asked in a high tone.

"He went back to his car after I told him I do not know you." The news shocked him but he was expecting something like this anyway. Instead of it breaking him, it drove up the adrenaline in him.

"Thank you," he replied and looked into their eyes and he could see the curiosity, but for him to be safe it was best not to say anything to them.

The broken pipe was nothing now. A bigger matter had arisen again. He was starting to work out his next plan. He was sure that if they got their hands on him, he was a dead man. He would only pray to see the next day. If you are in a war you cannot win, rather run and call it escaping to a new life. The only future for him here was a future six feet under; these man took advantage of the weak. "*The power of the oppressor is in the mind of oppressed.*"

He still believed in his freedom. "*This is what it has come to,*" he thought. Dealing with killers who lacked a simple conscience and sympathy, who would kill a child if it was to their benefit. If Foster had not saved him that moment at the riverbank, what would have been left for George to say?

Tinashe had used all the money he had for drugs. Now he had his hands in his empty pockets only to find a small cell phone. He gave it to one of his closest friends to go and sell. He told him, "Then we buy more meth". They would do anything for it. He waited as his thoughts went deeper to seek for a simple solution. Who was there to help him right now? Time was ticking as two went to sell the phone. He could not risk being outside there. He was sure they had a picture or something to show around to people and not everybody was going to protect him. As a crack head, everyone is against you. His life had a darker side. "I am too young to die!" The fear of death is poison. Last week, he was a nobody and not interesting but everything had changed within two days.

Being his own parent, trying to provide for himself, made him accept any sort of hassle. Now he understood that not all this was a coincidence. All of a sudden he'd got a father, and how had he become the one to run up and pick up those two bags? He kept on asking himself, "*Why they did not do it themselves?*" It was a set up from day one. Someone had been watching him for a very long time and it was someone who had a better answer to that question than he did.

What Tinashe did not know was that a conversation had taken place two weeks earlier in a restaurant courtyard. George had invited Foster to lunch.

"I have a person ready for the job, he will give you a hand," said Foster. He had chosen Tinashe specifically.

Tinashe was now sitting in a corner. A few minutes had passed but it felt like hours. He could not share with anyone, and his closest friends were safer not knowing anything. Early in the morning of the previous day he had been happy, but that was not the case on this day. It is not every day that Christmas comes around, but when it comes we open our hands wide to let the blessings flow. Whenever you are determined, choose between options and you might be lucky, but sometimes begging is the only way to put food on the table. So in this life, never judge anyone because you never know what it takes from you. Education is the key to success only if you are privileged. The community has a range of engineer, doctors, philosophers and others, yet it suffers from a lack of basic needs. The difference between being born without a cent or having silver cutlery on your table requires only God Himself to act in the right direction and at the right time.

Almost forty minutes had passed and he was getting impatient. Then on the toilet door there was a knock and a whistle. He stood up and removed the lock. They showed him the money, which was two hundred bucks. After he'd counted it, he gave them a fifty to show appreciation that they'd saved him, although they wondered, saved from what exactly? He followed them out as they looked around. Nobody seemed to notice, but there is always somebody watching.

Tinashe walked fast to the taxi rank that was not too far away. Before he got into a taxi, he amazed one of the pushers who saw him coming back for more stones so soon. Days had gone by without seeing him around and now he walked over to him and bought another zip lock bag.

He shared the stones with his friends who had accompanied him, and he gave them a new pipe to replace the broken one. They gave him back the money to buy more stones again. The weather was colder than usual so what he needed was a blanket although he could not afford to sleep.

He went into Peterson Taxis; he knew someone from there. He'd spent most of his childhood in Peterson. It made it easier for him; nothing would be strange except his coming back. He was a hunted young man, and he was going to face the consequences – or not. He was willing to take his chances and bet on it.

When he got into the taxi he took the last seat at the back of the vehicle. He did not want to be bothered by the other passengers during the drop off. Tinashe wanted to be the last to leave the vehicle, and he was not in a hurry. An ordinary day for others was an exceptional one for him. It had changed the course of his life.

He was high and his face fell off. He bowed his head close to his hands as they lay on top of his thighs and now it was only him and his thoughts.

In his search for Tinashe, George had managed to call Jadea, and make him and offer that he probably could not refuse. Jadea thought about George's offer to make him rich, since they had one common enemy. Jadea had a lot to win in this. He knew that one should take no bribes, for a bribe makes one ignore something that one clearly sees. A bribe makes even a righteous person twist the truth. He did not intend to betray his brother, but Joey surely gave him every reason to. He wanted someone to feed his grievances and to give him reasons to kill Joey. George and Jadea turned out to have different goals, and the only thing that had brought them together was Joey Morish.

Nobody had sufficient information about the whereabouts of Tinashe. Jadea got out of his car and walked into a building. He produced his ID for a security check and access. Security told him to take a lift to number twenty-six, but he used the stairs. George stood up from the couch to meet Jadea when he knocked on the door. Jadea thought maybe he would recognise this face, but it was very new; he'd never met him before. Quietly Jadea walked into the apartment and George offered him a drink. Business had begun as usual.

Sitting in the taxi, Tinashe was oblivious to everything. His thoughts ran up and down every second, just to remind him how miserable his life was.

He was trying to figure out if George knew about him and if it was because they were related that he wanted him dead, and if he still wanted him dead. Foster played a saint just to get what mattered to him and him only. Everybody turns out to be a poisonous viper beside the road and along the path. He hoped not to cross paths with these men any time soon. He was now going back to where his life had started.

Thinking about this all gave him a headache since it made no sense at all for a bus boy. He'd collected bags that carried the riches of a lifetime, but he had no idea what they'd contained.

Jadea had fallen for George's bait and they spoke again. As George and Jadea were in discussion, they started by talking about what was at hand. George's interest was to find the young person, and Jadea was looking for a way to trap Morish and this had become his only objective. Their ideas diverged due to different values and objectives, but they agreed to work together.

"I was with him, and actually I gave him a phone to call you…" Jadea said.

"Then why didn't I receive any call from him?" George asked.

"He knew about how you wanted him dead so it scared him away," Jadea replied. "Yeah, I was playing kit-kat," he added. "That is what happened. I could not force him to call, but I ended up pushing too hard."

George murmured to Jadea, "I do not blame him. This business of ours leaves you without anything, just like a drug addict."

"They do not have anything," said Jadea. "Are you definitely sure that he is your son?" This was a wise question that he asked.

Without doubt, George nodded. He knew he had forsaken the boy. He was sure money changes people and he'd had enough of it. For, from within, out of a person's heart, come evil thoughts, sexual immorality, theft, murder, adultery, greed, wickedness, deceit, lustful desires, envy, slander, pride and foolishness. He only wanted what was his and he simply pulled a bite to Jadea: about fifty thousand. He told him to use that money to find his boy and go back to the others. "Act like nothing happened at all. Otherwise, if they find out you're snitching on them they are going to slaughter you." These were George's exact words.

Jadea thought that this was a minor job, but the money given was much more than he'd expected. *"There must be more from where this is coming from,"* he thought. He had wondered who he should believe, but the money made him believe what he wanted to believe.

He took the money and left. This was just getting real.

Detective Mduduzi went block by block, searching for the boy. They had to go through shops with CCTV outside, but mostly it seemed to be not working properly or in seriously poor condition. These cameras were just scarecrows: almost seventy-five percent of them were not working, mostly in shops belonging to the Ethiopians traders. They lost hope in this searching as they had worked all day and it was actually tiring. They all decided to end the day. Pushing too hard will not bring out a good result and questions usually arise in that process. They had the following day to do this and additional officers on duty all night could carry on with it.

They separated after a long day and Joey and Petrus went back to Petrus' office. Mduduzi talked to Foster that night, but they were both out of ideas.

Petrus and Joey were done talking about police and crime, which was an exhausting topic. To replace it, they ended up talking about common commercials and then moved to the easiest topic of them all: national politics. They kept talking about how suddenly protesters were shot at in some of the countries with autocratic leaders, who rule by fear and suppressing people, increasing corruption which has ruined many countries from developing infrastructures, and new technology.

They left the office, and Detective Mduduzi took his phone charger since his phone had made warning sounds about the battery being low.

Joey Morish was dropped off at a rental building next to a huge mall with an expensive place to rent. Then he made his way out to buy airtime. He had some other business to handle that night and from that time it was easy finding out other schedules already made with new and old associates. He'd had another life before the previous two days. "Tomorrow, what time should I come and pick you up?" Petrus shouted.

Joey stopped him there and said, "Do not bother because I will meet you at your office," and he walked away.

After the detective had parked his car, he remembered a promise. He hated being caught up in his work rather than spending more time with his children.

"Oh, I am so stupid," he said to himself. What was happening around him was starting to separate him again from his children, like had happened a few years back.

Detective Mduduzi had something stuck at the back of his head. He could not figure out what it was and that was the end of it. But other buried thoughts of the first day he'd met George arose. They'd had different agendas, but money had brought them together.

They'd run into each after being introduced by mutual friends. They knew him back then as the registrar; he would write down a few notes on his notepad. Detective Mduduzi proved that the old strategy of dawn attack (*zvambakwedza*), borrowed from the army, was effective and later on he mourned the death of his senior detective who had threatened some bad people. The detective before Petrus had challenged his old friends to a power battle and he'd lost his life in it. He pledged allegiance but, as all alliances evolve, there was a scapegoat. He could not take the fault for anyone, although they had made him rich enough to afford early retirement. You cannot be a hero at your own friend's expense, so to avoid that they slaughtered him like an animal. A world of evil has only unconscious devils. Some would call it running, but he'd tried to escape to a foreign location to start a new life. It had been too late. He had opened the door when the devil knocked, thinking he could talk some sense into him.

It was the former senior detective who had placed Petrus on patrol as his delegate. After trusting him, he kept on promoting him from one position to another as he proved himself worthy of the promotion. He was making up his own rules and they bothered nobody. As a young officer – ten years ago – his superior had always told him that he saw potential in him.

In this way he'd opened his eyes wide open, as gangsters paved their way by paying for silence, which has become increasingly a habit all over. He sent them on different missions, just to make more money. A few years later, he was able to afford a very good car. He became an expert at finishing any job assigned to him. Just like every policeman, many temptations came his way, and he gave in to them.

It had been another normal day. He'd gone to a faraway harbour with his boss, for whom they were waiting so he could give permission to unload some foreign container. The shipment was unauthorised.

They were laughing and joking as they gossiped about what was happening back at their office. He'd seen another young man, a bit older than him, although they were both in their early thirties. They only nodded at each other, passing by. He kept on looking at him, observing his moves carefully. It seemed as if everybody knew him and respected him.

The young man was Josh, Joey's nephew, and they had their investigation underway. It was not a coincidence that he was snitching on others, and among those he snitched on was George. He detailed the last piece of information about where they were going to be and what time they were going to be meeting. Through that information, they made a breakthrough after discovering illegal weapons being smuggled. Joey knew about Josh's moves, but he supported it because it was also paving the way for him.

The darkness that had fallen on his door and had remained unnoticed was beginning to take whatever blessings he owned. It was a tip-off that had taken out all his team and he'd survived by grace. He was at the right place, just at the wrong time. He'd run into a deep shaft after shots had been fired from nowhere. Many died on the spot and those who ran into the shafts were hunted one by one by the police, until a lot of them had been found. They were shot, leaving, they thought, *no witnesses*.

But George survived the bullets of betrayal. They'd thought everyone was dead in the mineshaft that year, although they were not sure about how many bodies had been recovered. It was later on that the sergeant who had been leading the investigation was found dead, tied to chair and with a bullet in his skull.

The following year marked the promotion of Petrus to detective, replacing the old detective. They all thought George was the killer, but he was innocent until proven guilty. He was dragged through the courts and among bribed judges. He remained a suspect and they delayed other investigations they had. They all claimed the gun in his possession was used for murder and it was unlicensed. He never twisted his statements. For those six full years that he was in prison while the case was dragged out and in courts, he kept on telling them he was neither a vigilante nor a suspect, but a victim of a conspiracy that was framing him.

The judge asked, "Who might do such a thing? Tell me, Why would someone find happiness in that?"

He told them, "I am not a free man until I am as dead as the man I am being charged for murdering."

These were the thoughts circulating in Petrus' head on his way home. He almost went through a red robot. The promise was to go out with his kids but again he'd failed. He ordered pizza on the phone on his way home, just to ease them up. After all, they were angrily waiting for him to arrive home.

Chapter 7

Going back to where it all started was Tinashe. Many do not know that people who have witnessed the cold hearts of human beings are those who sleep in the streets, for they see evil clearly. On his errand to the only place he was more familiar with, he was sitting in his corner in the taxi, eyes swerving out through the taxi window, wondering about tomorrow's problems. The road lights can drive away all your thoughts for just few minutes, he learned. Some other passengers were holding their phones, entertaining themselves. He was ignoring all of that and he felt some form of déjà vu. It is true that time neither moves fast nor slowly. It can, however, feel very slow when you are moving fast and way faster when you are moving slowly; it is all in the mind.

He understood one thing: he was a conqueror of his fears and doubts. That is the only key to unleashing what is within us. Fear makes people scared of simple change.

"Change is one of the most difficult things that we face. However, change is inevitable. One reason we do not like change is that we get comfortable where we are.

"We get used to our friends, our job, and the place we live. In addition, even if it is not perfect, we accept it, because it is familiar. Moreover, what happens is that, because we are not willing to change, we get stuck in what God used to do, instead of moving forward into what God is about to do. Just because God has blessed you, where you are, does not mean you can just sit back and settle there. You have to stay open to what God is doing now. What worked five years ago may not work today. If you are going to be successful

and a conqueror one day, you have to be willing to change. Not every blessing is supposed to be permanent. Not every provision is supposed to last forever. We should constantly evaluate our friendships. Who is speaking into your life? Who are you depending on? Make sure they are not dragging you down, limiting you from blossoming. Not everybody is supposed to be in our lives forever. If you do not get rid of the wrong friends, you will never meet the right friends. Even for those who have already been blessed with what their hearts desire, power does not corrupt. Fear corrupts.. perhaps the fear of a loss of power."

Tinashe's power came along with confidence. The streets and drugs had drained his health away. He could not forget the bounty on his head, and he could not either celebrate escaped death because for him the war was not yet over. He was a boy born in a war, who grew up in a battle. Victory became his name.

His aunt was mad at him, but she was the only relative left to him and he was not even sure if they were really related. For that night, he needed most a blanket and a nice corner with no disturbances. Nevertheless, he hated this part of town so much because it carried too many bad memories, memories that reminded him of what had happened in previous years when his closest and only true friend had died. If he could write his name on the wings on a dragon, he would make it bold and beautiful.

His friend had had a prolonged sickness that had come and gone. It started as flu and was followed by a couple of unbearably painful headaches. Without timely medical attention – they could not afford any – it took time until his life was gone. They say that street life makes people stronger and resistant to random diseases, but that is only a myth because street people die each week, each month and each year without medical assistance, especially after consumption of very poisonous drugs for relief. A short life expectancy is a given.

Tinashe tried to overcome the feeling but it was just too much to bear alone and sometimes he thought, *"Death is easy because life is hard."*

Foster's injured shoulder was causing him much pain and it had stuck in his head. Pill overdosing had become habitual. He made his way to the hospital again; the same hospital that had the corpse of a victim in the mortuary, a victim shot by George the other morning.

Foster received a call on his way to the hospital from Jadea, who was on a scavenger hunt. Jadea told him that for a while there would be silence from him until he found the boy.

An elevator took Foster to the ground floor from the underground parking. He asked the receptionist about Dr Choo and she told him he had already left. "You just missed him," she said.

He could not stand the pain anymore; he needed someone's help quickly. The receptionist wrote down a room number on a small piece of paper and referred him to another doctor. This was his lucky day. Choo had powerful friends so he remained untouchable even in troubled times. The story about the victim was, bit by bit, starting to disappear. Many were just using it to source out information and wage wars with it.

Another thing that made him focus was the fact that he could not trust any constables anywhere. The fact remained that the evidence still pointed to him as a perpetrator. If he did not agree to their demands quickly, they were going to loop him out and make him a whipping boy, or a witness for a better sentence. This was part of the story which had made him stand back while Joey humiliated Jadea. He could not tell Jadea everything, how deep the mess was, because he would realise that George and he had many charges on the front line: attempted murder, murder, robbery, unlicensed weapons and more.

He went off to find the room that the receptionist had written down. The hallway had bright lights, the lift down right. He got into the elevator with two women. One was a visitor and the other one was a nurse with two blue folders in her hands. At the second floor he walked out of the lift, and two more people passed by, going into the lift.

Any evidence leading to him posed a threat. This was one of the reasons why his mind could not settle. He knew that either they had nothing at all to link him to what had happened that morning or, surely, the detective had something contradicting that. For so long he'd wondered when he was not going to be useful anymore. *What will happen then?* Words from his mouth were not powerful and could be used against him.

He walked down through the second floor hallway. He checked the paper for the extension number. Another nurse was coming his way and he asked, "Where can I find Doctor Marobe?"

Luckily, he'd asked the right person. She pointed him to the room. "It's pretty hard here to find a doctor or anyone in this big place," she said. She continued on with whatever she was doing and left him alone. Foster knocked on the door twice, and stood by the door. No response came to greet him. Another nurse was surprised to see him knocking on the door. She came and opened the door for him. He found the doctor in the middle of his work and quietly he walked to him. A signpost on the wall said:

NOISE IS PROHIBITED.

PETRUS GOT OFF THE PHONE with a pizza company. They told him his order would be ready in ten minutes. His thoughts divided into fractions, trying to figure out something. "*Who was it*?" He thought with concern. He mumbled repeatedly, "*Who was it suppose to be*?" It was a simple question, but it troubled him very much.

He recalled somebody who might have answers to these questions. His late boss had had a very close friend: the only problem was finding the man.

Nevertheless, he also realised how these two cases could relate because the same people were involved in both cases. This was still the same game. The players had just shifted to another stadium.

Not for a second did he think about the whereabouts of the young boy. His mind was too occupied with other issues. He had no idea about how to look for him. Chasing after him was just another problem. Tinashe had no identity documents beside a birth certificate.

FOSTER, ON THE OTHER HAND, knew the young boy thoroughly. He'd been the one to buy the phone from his friends and, knowing they had influence over the boy, he had implanted the idea of the journey through Tinashe's friends. Foster had sent him away in order to keep him safe from the many other snakes who were looking for him.

At least that allowed some peace of mind, although his aching shoulder had taken some of it away. After he was in the room, the doctor walked to him. At first, he could not see clearly, because the light was too bright.

The doctor had a deep male voice. "I suppose you were here to see Choo and you just missed him?"

"My arm is giving me hell on earth and I think there is another problem with it," Foster replied. He explained more, "After Dr Choo treated me yesterday, I could barely feel the injury but the pain is all I can think about right now. It is stuck in my head like a pack of cigarettes. I hope you can do something."

Without any further conversation, the doctor knew exactly what Foster was talking about. "Sit on this chair and let me take a look at it," he said. He switched on a closer light to see more clearly. The doctor removed the bandages. The wound was bleeding and oozing. "You might need me to patch it again and you actually need a long rest, if you want to heal quickly." The doctor grabbed his instruments and started fixing the wound.

People in the taxi started one by one getting off at separate stops. Tinashe was starting to enjoy his new comfort zone, although the darker it became, the more worried he was. He needed a place to stay for the night. The street corners were no longer comfortable at all. Once you have had a sweet taste of life, it changes you. He had to think of something. Six months ago, when he'd met Foster for the first time, his destiny had been twisted. God's ways are beyond misinterpretation. When you're lonely and lost, it makes you think that death is better than life.

Jadea clearly had set his new path. Soon after he'd left, George made a few calls to set up more Bin Ladens and Maddox, a team they had in mind to lend an extra hand. Everybody was now interested in the job and a lot of money was on the line. Those who'd heard about it uninvited, quickly jumped on the bus. They had no idea of what they were about to do and didn't care, just so long as the cheque came in.

While being hunted, George gathered three scavengers for a street hunt. Three people with dangerous criminal records were brought in: Blacks, Ano and Fabiano. George put his money to good use. These individuals could engage in any gunfight without any fear. Any time they could pull the trigger if necessary. George had thought of himself as scary until he'd met the three musketeers. He'd heard about them while in the prison.

Blacks was forty-five years old and suspected of killing his wife. The case lacked enough evidence but he remained the only suspect. As for kids, he had some out there looking for a father. Not to mention that his hit-and-run offences could almost fill up a church with kids. He'd been arrested and jailed many times. "What does not kill you, makes you a monster." Life had always found him a victim. He'd only finished primary school and had been a prisoner for as long as he could remember. His mother and father had been murdered in front of him by some unknown men who were looking for his rebellious brother.

Ano made his way up by breaking into uptown houses, looking for safes. He sold anything he got his hands on for a give-away price. He was in his early thirties, but his face was weary due to alcohol addiction; a full-time drunkard, he failed to quit it. Most of the money that he had was spent on women and alcohol. That was how he liked it.

Fabiano was the oldest of them, almost older than George was. Whenever they were on a job such as this one, he would lead the way. He stammered and, if you dared make a joke out of it, he would hit you with anything close to him. He had a very bad temper.

Now they were seated around a small table in one of George's rented apartments. Right away, they started discussing how they could find the young man. It felt as if his soul, once deleted and dead, had again resurrected. He focused fully on it. He never showed them his gun, although he thought that they were more scared of him than he was of them. They treated him with overboard respect. He took some of the money and gave it to them. He told them what Tinashe looked like, and what he had been wearing the last time he'd been seen. He sent them into the field as a search party.

George also sought to take care of Joey Morish for one last time. He was bothered by him so much that he could not stand him.

MEANWHILE, JOEY HIMSELF FELT THREATENED by everything and he could see himself sinking down the drain. After he'd been dropped next to the mall, he went to his rental apartment. He made a one week payment. He was sure the case would be closed by then. His wife told him she was coming to join him. He had disagreed with the idea, but she'd insisted. All she wanted to do was to be with him. He wanted new extraordinary resources, including trackers. He had to make few calls about it.

The limit of power that was set above his head made him feel like he was underutilised. His power with the police was limited, so he decided to launch a different operation. In doing so, he had higher prospects of luring George with bait. You only get one chance and, if you miss the shot, then run away. This might end with you losing reputation in the market or, worse, everything you ever built, including your own life. Ambitions and ego can be very dangerous if they go together.

Once he was in the building, he could not wait to get to the phone. As soon as he had sat at the table, he called Lisa's number first. They started talking, while in the hall some females were giggling outside.

"Hello," she said, on a very low note. "How are you doing today?" She asked this with worry in her voice.

"I am doing well for now," he answered and they kept on mumbling sweet words to each other.

After that call, which lasted about ten minutes, he made another one that lasted about five minutes. He was not so energetic with this one. During the call, he took the gun out of a pocket and hid it under a pillow where it was easy to reach. When he got off the phone, he checked to see that the gun was fully loaded. If you live by the gun, you die by the gun. You cannot afford to miss or otherwise you will be missed, forever lost.

He was a cave dweller probably. He had his eyes only on the money. His personal interest in it grew rapidly. Whenever he thought about it, he knew this would turn his life around and maybe he could fly into the sunset afterwards. Everything had changed and many people were starting to open ears and mouth. It was not an ordinary Bodiviar Empire family. They all wanted a piece of rib-eye steak, roast Rosa tomatoes and garlic aioli for a meal ticket.

He placed his gun under the pillow again and went to have a shower. He needed a warm, refreshing moment and then he would maybe read the daily newspaper too.

THE DOCTOR FINISHED PATCHING THE wound. He took out a paper and pen, prescribing a few medicines to ease up any pain during nights and days to come. Foster walked out of the room with a young beautiful nurse in front of him, and he closed the door behind him.

Walking out quietly, they did as everyone else was doing: concentrated on their own business. It was that one moment when two people cannot have a conversation and then it gets weird between them.

Now, not thinking further, he asked "How's the good nurse?" He reduced the tension.

With beautiful smile she answered, "I am okay, and you?" They started chatting, and she led him to a woman in her sixties.

"Here they are." She gave him some pills and injections from the medication shelves. She told him how to use them and, after that, he found his way out of the hospital.

WHILE ALL THIS WAS GOING on, Detective Mduduzi and his kids were enjoying pizza.

His son could not shut his mouth, telling his father what had happened, what he had missed during the course of the day. He talked about the soccer game and everything that followed. He kept on saying, "You should have been there, Dad". Somehow, it got to Petrus and he felt pity for himself in that moment.

The weather had become harsh all of a sudden, feeling colder than it was, as the clouds had covered the whole sky. Staying indoors was the only option for him to avoid family flu the following week. Blaming the weather also gave him a good reason to keep everyone inside. He was starting to get anxious about having his family outside anyway.

None of them could see the change except for his wife. She could see how withdrawn he had become. His son did not really care about all of that. During the game, his mother had waved from the benches and it had given him a better spirit. Now he asked for his mother's phone so that he could show his father the pictures they had taken while at the game.

"Mom, let me show him even the video that you took!" He looked more excited than the usual him. He was able to show his father what he was talking about. They both enjoyed watching it. He was not much of book lover like his little sister.

Then Anna went into the kitchen to prepare hot soup. Pizza was just not enough, especially after the radical change in the weather that night. They had switched the heater on and it was all warm.

Chapter 8

Tinashe fell asleep while sitting in the taxi. He had his hands wrapped around each other for warmth. He opened his eyes and found that the last passenger in the taxi was him. Nothing was exciting enough to boost any positive energy in him. It could not have been darker. Here, the bright lights of the city could not help at all. *"I am a motherless child,"* he thought.

George had fallen asleep with a T. V. remote in his hands. After the men had left the apartment, he'd drunk non-stop. He tried to figure out where to reach out for the boy. It was starting to torment him. The funny matter was that they had met in the previous days. Apparently, they had met in a devious situation. What made it worse were his thoughts. They had changed his heart in the blink of an eye. He saw that he was not a good father or a good person, no matter how much he tried to find even the smallest part that could assure him that he was wrong. *"My father is a monster."* It remained a tormenting thought. George asked himself when and how he'd lost his ways, after a good father had raised him by hard work and love.

Nobody was ever there to tell George's side of story, and every story has two sides. The process of change had begun in him, after he'd felt the emptiness, yet he'd had everything that could be desired. It was not enough, after all. The question of morals remained. Whatever we do in life, bad or good, it always finds a way to come back at us, ten-fold.

All these thoughts were crucifying him. He could not sleep at all. He woke up and placed the remote aside. He wrapped himself up next to his bed. He was tempted by another glass of whiskey, and then he took some shots until the whole bottle was empty. It was not healthy. He slept with one eye open.

TINASHE STILL HAD CRYSTAL METH and marijuana in his pocket. Life had other plans for him. He remembered someone who was going to be happy to see these two things: a drug addict and a student at a certain college who was addicted to crystal meth and, unfortunately, anybody who tried to talk him out of it would end up by giving up. He was always happy to see the "stuff", and you were welcome to live with him as long you had the "stuff". Tinashe would go to him for that night.

What he did not know was that it was not a coincidence how they met, but calculated maths to bring him closer to Tanya.

Tinashe had long forgotten where he was coming from. His focus was on where he was going. He took himself back in time, and before any deal was offered on the plate. *"Life is just too much to handle and I'm barely fifteen!"* He thought about it thoroughly. He was not going back. He needed money and he needed a lot of it. At first, it meant so much because he'd never had any, but all these people had made him lose his appetite after all the ruthless lies. Some wars are worth forfeiting, just to prepare for a greater one.

He did not fully comprehend that he stood in the mid-centre of the war. He had become the most precious shining stone for over twenty-four hours. He was an asset.

"I'VE NEVER MET THIS CHILD," said Joey Morish on the phone. "I could have been confident about it, but now I feel like we are dealing with a mythology," he exaggerated. "Possibly, if Foster can give a perfect description to the IT people, they can hook us up with something, and yet, such kids do not have any form of identity and some of them are refugees. It is going to be very hard for a thorough search but possibly we will work something out." He dropped the call.

He stretched apart his hands and it showed that he was tired, and he went back to bed. He only lay on the bed, meditating. He wanted to draw a finishing line but he found it impossible to know where to put it exactly. Something mattered more than all the fortune in the bags. It kept on giving him strength because that was going to be the end of his life, if he was not careful enough. His days were numbered, just like everybody else's.

PETRUS WAS PLAYING "DAD" AT home and it was almost bedtime. He knew his wife had a couple of questions to ask. Occasionally she knew, but this time everything was wrong. She could feel for her partner when he could not.

He kissed his baby girl for a good night's sleep. He switched off all the lights while doing a house check before going to bed. He had just come out of the shower wearing his pyjamas, ready to take a nap. Petrus switched on the television that he had previously switched off. He just could not miss the late night news programme, which he used as a mind refresh every night.

Petrus wanted to stop thinking about George for just a little moment. He was home and that is where he wanted his mind to be. After being a hero to the entire police force, he was not a hero to his kids, nor a husband to his wife. Missing his son's football game was a big thing and he knew it. Now, after he'd thought about it for a while, leaving the force was in his best interests. In his mind, he was sure that if they got their hands on the moneybags, he would leave and start his own security company.

They'd abused the force long enough and bribes had made him twist the truth until he'd got used to it. It was time to quit.

His wife was waiting for him. She thought maybe talking to him could be a relief. A pastor had once urged them to talk a lot while they were having marital problems. In a way she could feel the heaviness her partner was feeling; she saw it clearly. He sought peace of mind, and space was everything. He stared at the same old news bulletin:

violence, corruption and graduates making it. All day and everyday. It was not interesting. Then he started dozing while sitting on the couch. He knew that by that time she should have dozed off too, but she was also stubborn. She knew him well, that he was a smooth operator. He could get himself out of any situation by sweet talking her.

She'd once had an intimate relationship with someone else, but it remained a story that was too long to begin with. Ego caused hatred between Petrus and his wife's lover, personal hatred as such. They could not be in the same town at the same time.

He rose from the couch, making his way to the bed. There was trouble in the bedroom. She told him, "We need to talk". Those words meant a lot.

TANYA'S SISTER KNEW FOSTER AND they were very close. She would give Tanya money for school and clothes, but he rather used it to buy meth and told her everything was good. The security guards working at the flat that Tanya rented knew Tinashe. They were tight. They would allow him to come in from time to time and send him for tea. Proving his identity was unnecessary. He told them that Tanya had sent him to fetch something from downstairs. They were a bit surprised to see him around. "It has been a long time," they said.

The elevator was out of service. He used the stairs to go upwards. When he knocked on the door, he could hear loud speakers playing hip-hop music. He knocked hard more than four times. Eventually, someone came to answer the door.

"Hello, is Tanya around?" he asked on a low note. "Yeah, come in. I remember you," he said.

Tanya's height was twice Tinashe's and he had dreadlocks and a yellow complexion. They had marijuana everywhere in the house.

"I am happy to see you! That is dope!" he screamed, and to the next guy he said, "Dawg, you will not believe who's here".

Tinashe smiled and he knew he was good for the night. Tanya had friends around him from time to time. Most of them were doing drugs. What affected him negatively was the culture. He reflected the positive energy and focused on trying to be one of the top glamorous fruits. He wanted things that he saw in music videos, such as a good house, money, beautiful women, cars and ice.

They all sat on couches and some were playing T. V. games. Tanya, with his roommate Neil, sometimes rented out space for money to buy alcohol. Neil would leave them and go to the bathroom to sniff cat or cocaine on a toilet sink. He was not much of a crystal meth doer. Cocaine and cat were his babies.

Tinashe trusted these people a lot. They showed him extra love that he was not getting from anybody else. They did not care about a lot things about him, only the fast life lane. They made him feel free around them. When they asked how he was, he told them he'd been lost in the wilderness but he was back now. They all laughed. He knew somehow they would cover his back when needed.

"I'm in a deep mess," he told them, hoping they would be listening after smoking two joints. "I might need to sort this one out sooner or later." When the story sounded gangster-like or dangerous, they would all turn their ears to him. He took out the plastic bag of meth, and showed Tanya. He told him, "I got one for the night".

How extremely excited Tanya was in a moment. Seeing those crack stones made him very happy. He said, "Thank you, bro".

Tanya asked Tinashe, "Are you leaving?" thinking he might leave with the stones, but he was unaware of the programme.

Tinashe lowered his face and exaggerated a sad feeling. He replied quietly, "You know me. My house is a street corner, tomorrow also. If it is okay with you, can I stay here while we are smoking? Only if it is okay with you."

Quickly, he replied, "No Dawg, you can relax and I am cool with it, and also even tomorrow you can stick around."

"Thanks man. I really appreciate that," he said.

They walked out onto the balcony and started smoking cigarettes and more joints. Tanya remained behind, creating a music play list, then joined them. They passed the *skiff* around. They would have arguments about music artists from time to time, and this was what they enjoyed most.

After they had finished smoking, Neil was in the house. Tinashe joined them as they walked downstairs to the public showers and the toilets. These toilets had no air coming in or out. Therefore, they had a poor ventilation system installed in them.

Two individuals were set to start smoking meth. Tanya took out the tube safely. It was the same kind as the one Tinashe had dropped earlier. Tanya took some stones and placed them inside the funnel-shaped tube. Before they started smoking it, they melted the crystal; solid into liquid. When they started smoking it changed from liquid to gas. It evaporated so fast that they kept on craving for more. It lasted for five minutes and then the rocks were finished.

FOSTER REALISED HIS HEADACHE WAS gone. He felt hungry but he had no appetite for any food, or perhaps he was just being lazy about cooking. Sometimes he would just buy take-away to avoid standing in the kitchen. The doctor had told him that he needed to eat before taking any medication. He went into the kitchen and grabbed a juice; it was enough for the night. Tinashe had eaten all the prepared food in the fridge. It was not necessary to think about him, but resting was surely necessary.

The morning was cold and windy. At 03h30, George was awake and sitting on a kitchen chair. Nightmares haunted him and he just could not find comfort in the liquor. The future can happen but it starts by leaving the past. As much as he wanted to find the young man, he was just dragging too many people into this. There was also the fact that he was spending money on non-professionals just because they knew the streets better than anybody else did. It was not helping at all. The more it went viral, the more someone was just going to grab the opportunity to kidnap Tinashe and make money out of it. This was his consideration.

He made a call to Fabiano to cancel their participation in this. At first, he had made a call out of desperate thoughts to bring them in, but these were killers. He thought of the money he had given them. It was going to waste away due to a silly decision and they would not refund. He asked Fabiano if they had made progress by any chance. They said they would not interfere but would rather keep a distance and a very close eye. They would not scare the bird away.

George opened another bottle of whiskey and iced it, under pressure, getting drunk. When you play a game, you play to win. He sat on that chair waiting for sunrise, which marked day three after the robbery.

He had flashbacks of busting bodies and anything for money. If this time anything bad were to happen, that was the end of him. He'd be lucky if they did not shoot him on the spot. Two of the bags they'd stolen contained two small pockets inside. They came from a place nicknamed "Southern Side" and they carried heavy weight. The small pockets had the most expensive carats in Africa: black diamonds. To get one, you had to be a very corrupt politician or someone who was extremely dangerous and rich. Just knowing about them is a bounty on your head, and your family might well never see you again. In most cases, soldiers carry out the brutal duty.

These black diamonds are smuggled into markets by every means necessary. For nearly a decade, diamonds helped keep Côte d'Ivoire a divided nation. Every year, rebels smuggled about twenty million dollars' worth of diamonds into neighbouring countries, exchanging these diamonds for weapons and strengthening their grip on the north. In 2004, a violent civil war in Côte d'Ivoire reached a stalemate. Rebels controlled the diamond-rich north while the government controlled the south. Bans were lifted on Côte d'Ivoire's diamonds in 2014. For the first time in years, the country had a chance to use its diamond wealth for peaceful economic development. Nevertheless, memories of war, and the destructive power of diamonds, will not soon be forgotten.

George was petrified, but fears and doubts had no place in his heart. He was a failed father because of his selfish agendas but this time he was not going to fail again, he was determined. "*After having got all this treasure, what was the end goal?*" he would ask himself.

God had given him another chance, so he picked the motivation.

It was 04h00 when he received a call warning him to leave the apartment and the caller told him they were coming in loaded for combat. He quickly jumped out of the chair.

Chapter 9

There was not enough time for him to grab everything. He grabbed what he could and fled. When he left the place, it looked deserted. He had one big bag with everything in his car. At that moment he had his eye glasses on, blue jeans and a white silk shirt.

He only had about ten minutes to move out but he did it in five. He drove out of the garage very quickly. It was an unexpected dawn attack by men at work. He'd managed to escape by the skin of his teeth. Soon after he'd left, they arrived on four wheels. His car had travelled about half a kilometre when he stepped out of the car and looked back. He could barely see them because it was dark and he was intoxicated. He wanted to see who they were.

Finally, he had relaxed and calmed down, so he got back into the car. He started driving back to the storehouse, which was known by Foster as his warehouse. Foster had planned to abandon it because he was sure it was no longer safe, but it was going to take him two working days to shift everything. That was as far as he could go and hide out while planning for his next charge. Everything he'd planned so far was water under the bridge. He thought maybe from there he could use his laptop to see every change that was happening in the market.

Just like what once happened in stock broking firms and markets, brokers were manipulating the market to suit their needs. It was a most tragic profit-making game. He was sure that he could not be traced to the warehouse and he hoped not to run into Foster; they still had unfinished business. What he had left at the apartment was nothing that mattered to them. *The best place to hide is a place where you are least expected to be.*

When they got to the apartment, they turned it upside down. They searched everywhere, thinking that maybe he'd heard them coming in and had hidden himself. Little did they know he was long gone. "How did he know that we were coming?" they asked each other. A glass still had ice melting in it. They looked in every corner, but they only found a holy bible laid on the table, opened at the book of Psalms, Chapter 23. They had come well prepared, with dozens of guns and tear gas. Joey was furious and he exclaimed, "Next time we are going to get closer than this!"

He called someone while standing in the midst of the room. Others were wearing gloves, searching thoroughly for anything but being careful not to leave their fingerprints lying around. He calmly talked to the person during the call. "We missed him and we missed by only a few minutes." How long does ice take to melt in a whiskey at about room temperature?

It took about thirty minutes to wrap up and leave the place.

George was not sure about who had snitched on him but he told Fabiano to lay low again. He told them he was not making any collaborations at all. He knew the whole city wanted him.

The third day, 07h00

MORISH DID NOT WANT TO lose Detective Mduduzi's loyalty and he knew that what would bother him was being left in the dark. He called him that morning and told him about the failed attack.

George had reached his destination. Now his thoughts and the liquor had given him the courage to face whatever war they would bring to his door. He knew this was not about the victim and the accusations. It was all about the money. *For a rich man to enter heaven is harder than for a camel to pass through the eye of a needle*. Whatever was going to come, it would find him there.

He was negotiating a price with a buyer on his well-protected laptop. He was surely untouchable and these individuals were as terrified as anyone could possibly imagine. He knew them by name and he could come after each and every one of them. He told himself at last that he was no more than a bandit was, especially if he kept on running from place to place. "I am here to stay."

None of them was as innocent as they claimed to be. The truth is that, whatever happens, you have to determine your stand.

UNFORTUNATELY, WHEN HE GOT TO the warehouse he could not stay as anticipated. Something was not adding up. George was no-longer sure, so he closed his laptop and left the area. He knew sooner or later his face would be all over the place. He was no longer feeling secure and was always paranoid. He closed the place and went to the other side of the city, a suburban area.

Around eight o'clock, he was in the city searching for another hotel to stay in for a while. Money was not a problem but it brought problems. He stuck to his plan of staying hard to get and avoiding being sensitive.

TANYA HAD SMOKED SOME OF the meth and they could not sleep at all. They talked a lot until they ran out of stories. Tinashe started preaching to them his story. He told them what was happening in his life.

At midnight, they travelled to the warehouse and broke the lock. However, when the alarm started to make a noise it did not take Tinashe long to switch it off.

DETECTIVE MDUDUZI WOKE UP WHEN he received Joey's first call of the day. He had a glass of water and all the depression had faded away from his face. Being calmed down by his wife overnight was not enough to stop the situation at work. His reputation and money were on the line. It was a great morning indeed; everything seemed to be coming closer and closer to him.

It was after Joey's call that he saw another missed call from a warrant officer. He called him back. There was some new evidence that might bring this case close to the end of its era, which meant bringing George to the light and he would be a real hero. It brought joyful music to his ear.

He began the day by driving his children to school. They were having all kinds of arguments that he would not intervene in. He kept on driving quietly. One of the reasons he kept quiet was that his mind was occupied by questions of respect and loyalty. "*Why was I left out from the mission carried out by Joey?*" His thoughts were nearly driving him crazy. He was the number one leading detective of this investigation, yet he had been left out when the real investigation was carried out. He wanted to put a bullet in George's skull himself.

Joey as always had a good reason for why he'd done it alone. He'd said that one of the reasons was that he did not want to disturb Petrus and his family in the evening. Petrus asked more questions. His instincts insisted that something new was going on. In other words, it was a great morning indeed.

Joey applied for one of the offices in the station, so that they could do their own work separately, as in carrying out research and so on. Some of the people he was working with were not as persevering as he was. Since they'd started, they had been throwing evidence away. He reached the conclusion that starting over again in a proper way and not cheating his way through until he got his quarry would be best.

Petrus had dropped his kids off, each at their school, starting with his little girl. He walked into his office and found new cases that had arisen, all waiting for his attention. From everything that had happened during the previous night, he was sure the current case had made a breakthrough after the crackdown. They knew somehow, someone would be a witness.

One of the officers walked in after him while he was doing his daily routine: opening windows and checking his daily schedule. Sometimes classical radio channels were good as a day starter.

"Good morning, Detective," the officer said. He was one of the officers carrying things out the way an officer should, without a different agenda. "We have a new witness."

He replied, laughing, "What is this new witness claiming he knows that we haven't heard already?" Petrus sat on his office chair.

"He claims to have seen the car leaving the same area, the same time, after the crime and says he could recognise it if he comes across it again."

This, although Detective Mduduzi did not know it, was the same car that Tinashe, Neil and Tanya had stolen earlier in the morning. He knew the description of the car. If they were to find it, it would lead them to the right owner.

"Who is this witness anyway? I hope he is not just some street sleeping scant." Actually, he could not care less about anything other than to see Joey and his new companions. He was eager to know the next move.

Joey was with the Colonel at that moment. The Colonel urged him to set aside some of the information and keep him well informed. Orders from above were putting Joey under pressure. He asked for his own keys to the office, as if he had just turned twenty-one. Luckily, he received them with pleasure. He'd told the Colonel that he felt like he was not welcome without them.

AROUND NINE O'CLOCK, FOSTER WAS just coming out the shower when two men knocked on his door again. Joey's forbearance had run out. Joey needed answers and people, also to set up his allegation straight and strengthening his interview strategies. The more time Joey spent doing nothing, the more time George had to slip away. All this did not matter to him, what mattered most was if the gun was loaded with fourteen bullets.

George's heart and mind insisted, "*Let this go*". That type of freedom was not available, however. He would remember being trapped in the mine all those years back. His skeletons were determined to come out of that mine. The many killings, including the death of the detective before Petrus, made him a target. That detective had gone down as a hero, but he was not a saint at all and his cupboard was full of bones. George had killed many people but he was not, in fact, guilty of killing a former detective. That he'd been accused angered him and hurt him so much that he could not forgive. "*Anger is the most impotent of all passions. It affects everything it touches and hurts the one who is possessed by it more than the one against whom it is directed.*"

Before the detective had been murdered, he'd spent a lot of time trying to strip George of his power. The way he was on him was like the eye of a vulture from miles in the air, spying on a dead animal. The person who had actually killed him was, however, trying to shut him up forever. The former detective had been going wild with his mouth, saying things that he'd once given an oath to keep secret. He would be alive if he had just agreed to keep taking the bribe and let everything slide. He'd created and written his own destiny. Many people were scared, for it was not looking good for them.

The time he'd done behind bars had made him tougher with his approach to these people. These diamonds had caused successful nations to fall because of greedy individuals. Innocent lives had been sacrificed because of them. Many were still pursuing them to make themselves richer, using these minerals in ignorant ways. Many young African children being born nowadays have no idea about the treasure they are walking on top of, of what Africa is supposed to be. And, as we watch it, our elders are stripping away the honour they once fought for. Yet they divide attention and create many groups that sabotage unity, for example based on skin colour, and to see what is in front of one's nose requires a constant struggle.

George clearly realised he had become a super villain. He asked himself, "*Was it worth all the money? I have so much yet I cannot find anywhere to be at home and constant love that is unconditional.*" Inner peace is so expensive that it cannot be bought with money.

Many had recognised that the previous detective and George were reaching the limit of their usefulness. George's vicious thoughts about a vast, notorious revenge recognised that some people would turn against each other. When that happened, he would stand by and watch how it went. After they had cancelled each other out, he would come in as a new saviour.

He picked up his phone to make a call to one of his oldest friends. He had all the information inside and out. This was the same person he had tried to get in contact with over the previous two days. He knew they could dig up some information for him as a special service.

FOSTER, WHO HAD LOST HIS big ticket, was disappointed. He'd been convinced that he'd chosen to work with the police just to reclaim what was his and that they had the same interests.

Joey Morish only wanted those stringed pockets.

Detective Mduduzi only had an idea of what was in the bags, and he was not sure how much it could amount to. So much was laid on the plate for him.

TINASHE ASSUMED THAT THE BAGS were priceless, but knew no more than that. He poured out his words to Tanya and Neil. Neil spent most of his time robbing safe boxes. "Do you know of any safe?" he would ask. They could not believe what Tinashe was saying, but later they started understanding him when they saw the tears. They had sat that night listening quietly and attentively. There were no more jokes. Then they had gone out and stolen the very vehicle that Foster had used as a getaway car.

When George moved to the heart of the city he had a place to be. His old friends had agreed to dig up the information he needed most. The word on the street had become so bold that few people knew what was happening. It was not something for social media. The word reached to the so-called owners whose property was in George's hands. They told Joey to handle it quickly, as usual. They had known for some time that he could get the job done in time. However, this was not just some junk person drug addict, but a long-time friend. Joey had decided to stay close and watch out for snakes.

Knowing that running away would not solve anything, George went to a simple three star hotel. He left his car in the garage, which was located under the hotel. He never looked closely at the cameras. Someone had taught him how to get his hands on a CCTV's control cable. Whatever they could see in the operating room, he was well aware of. He'd learned many corrupt things during his time of living, experience that he had used since the beginning of all his operations and that allowed him to be extra careful.

It was time for payback for the lost time. He'd reached out to some people through phone calls. He had a lot of money and it was time to put it into real use. With the kind of money he had, he was able to buy people. There were those who were the hunters. As long you were still using your ordinary identity they could find you anywhere because they were everywhere. They brought nothing but trouble.

Now he was hunting them, instead of them hunting him. He was going after them all. He had become a city hunter. *"One thing that money buys from people is respect. If it's blood-stained, people will love you even more for it."* After taking a shower, he would come up with a new idea. *"All eyes on me,"* he thought.

Joey was with the detective, giving him strategies on how they could move towards George. While they were still talking, Jadea walked in surprisingly, and his face looked as if he had stumbled on a rock. Joey was fascinated and stunned. Still in shock at seeing him, he stopped listening to what the detective was preaching. Jadea feared not, for he believed he was still of vital use to the search. He'd rather get fired than quit.

"I was not expecting to see you again!" Joey exclaimed. Detective Mduduzi offered him a seat on the other side of the couch. He did not let Joey annoy him but it happened again. He only ignored it and courageously it gave him more reason to do what he had come for. The right words flew out of his mouth.

"Joey, just think as if we have met in the street after a very long time without seeing each other. No offense taken I hope," he said. "This is how I pay my bills," and while they were still in a chit chat, Foster had arrived with two policemen and it seemed like he had been forced out of bed.

When Foster walked in, they all had their undivided attention focussed on him. They knew one thing: he was the one who still had fresh wounds and that is why they needed his anger around. None of them wanted this more than Foster.

"Speak of the devil and he walks right in," Joey told them. He was now surrounded by about seven people and he was the eighth. "Another day has begun, gentlemen," he told them. "We almost had George today."

Now Jadea and Foster looked at each other in surprise. A silence broke out. "My hands are still empty, and his eyes are everywhere. Perhaps even here, who knows?" He laughed, easing up the tension between these men. He turned to Jadea and apologised for any inconveniences. "We might have got off on the wrong foot and I am truly sorry about that. My anger sometimes overwhelms me. I hope to work together. Let's set aside personal interests and focus on the goal."

They all agreed with him.

He turned to Foster and asked about his shoulder. "Just remember, a killer is on the loose. Are you willing to die for anybody else?" he asked.

"Since we are all here, let us do some catch-up. The detective's office has become a bit small for all of us!"

They all laughed with fake smiles. They were all ready to set aside their differences. Just get it over with. They'd agreed to it, but surely deep down hatred was still between them.

Foster asked, "What was the last place you spotted him?" He meant George. Then Joey reached out his hand to grab a file. He could not speak aloud about it and the question Foster asked remained hanging.

Chapter 10

Mbali experienced a moment of pleasure. He felt the rise within him. After all, he had not been given a chance to speak after his surprise arrival early that morning. He was one of the three mighty people Joey had taken from the force to help him out here. Joey had always admired his spirit, reasoning capacity, and how thoughtful he was in such things. Mbali could give orders as a delegate. He spoke of giving others a wakeup call. He took out his tablet phone and started reading out information to everybody. From the information provided, it was clear that something was hidden and was only meant for certain ears.

"We have traced him, right from the place he shot Foster." At first, it was not clear, like during a cloudy, cold winter. "This morning was supposed to be the last time this was discussed, but the target is not just some ordinary individual. He knows all the tricks. We checked everything and everywhere but, like Osama Bin Laden, he creates tips before you. He is playing us. The camera from the opposite building never picked him up, or perhaps it did and he just manipulated it, just like every camera we have spotted at the apartment building."

Then he urged them, "He's got connections everywhere so rather keep what you know to yourselves and open your ears more. He might be using a Grand Cherokee and we just confirmed it now. Someone did identify something like that one in the city. We have somewhere to start now."

Not everybody was buying it. Foster was thinking about Tinashe more than about capturing George. He knew nothing was in it for him, if they were to capture George. Surprisingly he felt better when they did not mention Tinashe at all. He needed his own separate advantage. "Let me visit all my connections. Maybe they can give me answers," Foster said.

"No," Joey replied. "I need you close if I get hold of George and that is why I sent them to retrieve you like a document!"

All through this, the detective was quiet, just trying to read each and everyone's face and he kept on looking at Jadea, asking himself this question over and over: *"Why is he back here after the way he was treated?"*

They separated into different groups and Mbali went off with his team. Joey wanted to spend the day with Foster on the side. He was the only one who knew exactly what was going on with everything. It was a lie that this was not about those stones. Feelings aside, work proceeds.

Jadea did not leave but stayed behind in the office with Detective Mduduzi. Petrus suspected something was going on but what that was was not accurate. The relationship between Foster and his cousin Jadea was business based but, as they told each other, after being through many things together they would not let business come between them. Therefore, everything was all good.

Joey knew Foster was never going to stop searching for George and he wanted to know where he was. His relationship with George was beyond repair.

THE YOUNG BOY HAD ESCAPED death from a gun. Hardcore was all he'd ever wanted to be. Now he found himself with a very nice car, and he was sure that no one was about to press charges about its loss.

The car that they had stolen was parked elsewhere. As for them, they were all still lying in bed. By that time of the morning about eight hours had passed since they'd taken it from the warehouse and they no longer felt that high, although they could still sense it. They'd parked the car in an abandoned building that was next to the building they were living in. They knew how to get in and out without being noticed. It was one those places they smoked in. While they were still in the car it was lucky that they did not run into any police patrol car, or they would have been in big trouble.

Tinashe kept on insisting they would sell the car. He kept on reminding Tanya and Neil that this car was used to commit a serious offence and if they were to be caught with it by either the owner or the police, it was the end of the game. Therefore, he suggested they should sell the car and use the money from it to start their own business.

What they said was nothing serious because they were crack heads. Tinashe was not even sure if their points were worthy of being valued. He was sure of one thing, they would do anything for money.

Before they went to sleep they'd decided to deal with the car problems, including selling it, during the day. Although they did go to bed, they could not sleep well because of that car.

Tanya woke up first and shouted with excitement. "Let's go and take a look at our new baby!" The three of them were awake but, as usual, they started their day with a smoke before anything else. They went to the other side of the building while smoking a joint. The security guards that usually patrolled around the area would smoke with them from time to time.

At first they'd stopped them when they'd gone into the restricted buildings in the area and had asked them, "Why are you going into this building? Don't you know it is restricted?" They always brought weed with them and that would make up for everything.

Today, when they were walking into this building, one security officer saw them and he was never the smoking type. "Wait here," Tanya said, turning his back to talk to him.

"Hold on." Neil followed Tanya and left Tinashe. He took out about twenty bucks and gave it to the guard, which was more than enough for what he needed. They went into the building. The argument started again, when Tinashe raised the topic once more. At last they agreed to search the car. Maybe they would find something of value.

Now they opened all four doors. This car's black market value was about a hundred thousand bucks. They started playing deep hip hop from one of the CDs they had found in the car. They looked for any fault but could not find any. Neil was inside searching for whatever he could find under the seats. When he opened the dashboard and found a loaded revolver inside he took it and hid it quickly, before his friends noticed it. When he checked again in the same place, he also found a few hundred held together with rubber bands.

Tinashe was virtually illiterate, so he ignored all receipts and paper, giving them to Tanya. Tanya was in college, although he barely attended his lessons.

Now that the car was in their hands, there was more to be expected from them. They were also scared that this car had been used for a robbery that had resulted in murder and selling it was going to be a small problem, but they could deal with it. Going to jail was the last thing they wanted to do. Tinashe's day troubles were over and he could handle anything. He felt like a young king.

JOEY HAD ONE OF THE official government cars to use. He was with Foster when another car ran into them. Some young fellows were speeding along and shot through a red robot. The car was damaged on the front side. They could not go anywhere at all. The two cars had crashed into each other, but the accident had not caused any sort of damage to the passengers. The red car that had run into them went on to hit another signpost at another corner as a result of the driver's panic. Luckily, the two people, in their early twenties, who were in the car did not get hurt but what had happened was going to give them more problems than they were already in.

Joey got out the car angry. He was waving his hands around and shouting. He walked over to them and said, "I advise good lawyer fellows for you."

The young fellow who was driving realised that he was on the wrong side of the law. They wanted some sort of reconciliation without going to the courts. If the car they had hit had been Joey's car, of course the insurance would have taken care of it and he might have gone easy on them, but unfortunately it belonged to the government. They had bumped into the wrong car.

Joey was calm but the fact that this had happened in the middle of something very important and the young fellows seem intoxicated meant that it was not going to end well for them. Ten minutes later, police had arrived at the scene and two breakdown trucks had also arrived. One was white and black and the other big truck was painted orange and lime. They parked behind one another just after the intersection. Joey's car was in the middle of the intersection. The other car was just against the corner signpost pole. On a busy working day, they had caused many traffic problems, since it was one of the main roads into the city. Joey was talking to the police in the front line and he showed them an identification card.

He told them to deal with the case quickly as it was time for him to leave. Their car could still go on. Joey drove to the closest police station.

WHEN HE LOOKED AT THE back seat of his car, Jadea remembered the jacket Foster had given him to give Tinashe. Jadea and Petrus went back to where he'd lost Tinashe. Maybe on a different day when the pressure was low, he could try to find him. They took another turn at this search. There were many of them and they were able to divide into specific groups. They did not have a strong working relationship but they were working towards the end goal better and better. They had rounded up all the young boys on each corner who were the same age, height and appearance as the young man they were seeking. They drove to see each of them, hoping they would get lucky, but the heavens were tight.

George had relaxed and took out a phone, transferring some of his contacts into a new phone. While he was sitting right there, something struck his mind. A story about a man who practised unlimited faith until his freedom came. George's old friend had once told him about this man.

"A man was convicted of murder charges but he denied these charges and justice was served anyway. Since the first day he was taken to a cell and in the seventeen years that followed he did something very annoying to the other inmates but it was just an act of great faith. He would wake up each morning of those seventeen years behind bars and sing a glorious song to God. As soon as the song was done, he would shout, "Lord Jesus Christ is my saviour". It got to the point that other prisoners hated him for it. Usually they would throw anything they could, including spoons and trays. However, he never stopped and he became an alarm of the prison.

When George had heard this story, he'd admired the courage of this man to make such a commitment in such a place.

After spending a very long time inside, this man went for a hearing, but to grant him parole they asked him, what was the truth behind everything? They thought maybe after all these years, his mind was upright about the allegations. He told them for the last time that he'd never committed the offence, so they denied him again.

After this, it got even rougher for him and they were torturing him. He felt a deep depressions when they told him his wife had died. It was a way for him to give up and give in his free spirit. No matter how bad things were, though, he did his daily routine. On the devastating day that he was told about his wife, it was around 8PM when the lights went off. Guards had taken one of his wife's pictures during the time he was at the hearing, so they dressed a random girl in the same way as his wife was dressed in the photo. With the wig and dress, she passed along in front of his cell and he thought he was hallucinating. He believed his eyes and quickly moved close to the front bars, but he could not see her anymore. He was sure that was her… or maybe he was going mad because of her. Instead of tormenting him, it made him stronger and he understood she was still alive, against all the odds.

His case was so serious that he was on the list of those who were facing execution. This prisoner execution process was usually done in the eyes of other prisoners. It was exactly the way they wanted other prisoners to know that the prison system was still merciless. A few weeks passed while he waited for the day of execution. Two days before, they took him out of the prison cell. All the prisoners had planned to rise up with their hands up high, just like he had done over all the years that had gone by. They all started singing the same glorious song the day they took him.

Out of nowhere, someone from the courts came to tell the prison officers to take him out. He told them that this man's charges were wrong. The man's life had been tormented for a very long time on false accusations. At last, the true light reviewed him as honest. All he'd needed was patience but it had been very painful for him. Some lives are chosen for different matters than the usual.

TANYA WENT ON HIS PHONE application and started inviting some friends to come over. These friends were girls and he invited about five just to be sure, in case two of them did not show up. It was a great day for the boys. They walked out of the building, leaving the car safe and secured. Tinashe's clothes were all dirty. He felt like it was normal in them. He was used to it, but now he wanted to buy new clothes. Everybody was after him and he decided to take his game up high. He found a gap and ran through it.

FOSTER'S SOUL BELONGED TO JOEY. He was in a tough position to make decisions. This gave him more energy and it was driving him more to get the stones. They wanted all the credit for themselves and they had promised him nuts in return. He'd once thought his injured shoulder was an obstacle but now he realized that it was his reminder and strength altogether. Everybody dies some day, some happy and some upset, but the one who dies for a cause is greater than many.

It was about six months earlier that Foster had come across George, who had approached him about a job. George was fully aware that he might have a son out there. Foster was the one who'd said to him he would look into it, that he was sure that this might be true. It was just after George's release from the jail when everything came through.

George had pleaded innocence on the cases and surely his hands were clean. That one case proved them wrong, but he had been a cold-hearted killer at some point in his life. The devil grows in the hearts of the selfish and wicked; white or black, the colour is not restricted.

At the same time that Foster promised to find his son for him, George explained about the specific deliveries on marked dates that happen twice a year. Even while he was in prison, he'd monitored each of those twelve trips that were made over the entire six years. He'd noticed the same activity. He had eyes everywhere and some wanted him out for their sake.

He'd once tried using someone to do the job for him, but eventually it was a failure. Someone controlled this operation with such strict rules that the pick-ups and drop offs were done during midnight hours. George took a complete check up and recognized it was still the same process. It had a code name: *Evaporation System.* Evaporation system was the extraction of the diamonds from the source or the local buyers, condensation was collecting them into one place and, lastly, precipitation was supplying them to customers. George later on told Foster about the previous life he'd once had and the places that he'd met various women, including Rose.

THOSE MONTHS THAT HAD PASSED also marked the time that Tinashe met Tanya after he had lost his best friend. He was actually standing next to a sneaker shop on a corner. Some individual who worked in a close-by salon as a barber would give him marijuana to sell at that corner. Tanya became one of his regular customers.

Tanya would journey up and down the stairs more than three times a day, just to get hold of that smoke. Sometimes the barber would lay low when the police started smelling the dead meat about the activities at the corner, but sometimes they would not believe it because of the age that was hustling the drugs out. When everything was low, Tinashe begged for money or anything to eat. If you wanted to buy him food, he suggested something like bread that would last longer.

Tanya's life was driven by peer pressure most of the time, until he became *peer pressure* itself. Life almost dragged him everywhere and he followed.

Once, when Tinashe was not selling, Tanya bought about ten packs of marijuana and gave seven to the boy to sell. He motivated the young boy to stay put and alert. He said that his eyes would be opened, as much as he knew these streets better than everybody else did. When he gave him those seven packs, he told him that around 10PM they would meet and when they did, Tinashe should give him the money and they would split it in half. That night, Tinashe never came back. Another day went away and Tanya kept on waiting. He even went to check him in all his spots. Tinashe had lied to him and never came back to meet the agreement they had. He wondered why he had trusted him anyway: *block dealer*.

They met again after many days had passed. Tinashe gave him a good explanation that was nothing else but another lie. That day he was standing against the sneaker shop when Tanya approached him. He told him someone was holding his money for him. While they were still talking, someone came up to Tinashe and gave him ten bucks. Tinashe walked towards the end of the shop that separated it from the next shop. There he had hid some marijuana in plastic under two bricks. He left his customer standing with Tanya. He came back with it and gave it to the customer.

They went to Tanya's apartment later that day. That was the beginning of their friendship. Tanya's sister was responsible for his bills, including paying fees, food and accommodation, as he was barely studying Business Management. He had dropped the number of modules, so that he could have more money left in his hands.

He tried to work but, after working for two or three months, he would quit and complain about mistreatment at the place of work, but actually he was missing working days while doing meth, sometimes even more than a week. He was not much of a drinker; rather meth was everything. One time he got employed and he started talking sense about how much he wanted to buy his daughter new clothes to wear or do something that could help her but, as usual, he failed to keep the money and used what he had earned to buy stones.

JOEY AND FOSTER EXCHANGED THE damaged car to go and meet up with the usual executives and black market lords who knew everything about hot diamonds. That was the first place for George to go and it was a very well known place because big major players and partners who were anonymous at all times protected it.

"Do you think he has yet tried the market place?" Joey asked Foster out of desperation.

Foster replied to him, "There might be a chance that he did. This is the only place to make such a dangerous exchange." They were both fully aware of a place that was located inside of a club. "Let's go to meet these old friends of mine," he said. The car accelerated. Foster had long forgotten that he needed rest but, because of money, that was next to impossible.

JADEA WISHED WORDS TO APPEAR on the paper giving him the directions for finding Tinashe. If Detective Mduduzi Mduduzi found Tinashe on his search, he would be the happiest man. They had made a drawing of Tinashe and had printed many copies of it. He knew that he remembered the young man's face perfectly. His phone made him think about it. Jadea recalled how many nudes that different women, including his baby mother, had sent in the stolen phone. It was just an embarrassing thought for them to been seen by someone else. He would not even show such images to his best buddies.

They'd collected about eight boys and none of them was Tinashe. However, one of them was Makhathini, who knew Tinashe in and out because they had been friends for so long. When they asked them if they knew him, they all denied it at once, including Makhathini. They let all of them go, but Makhathini returned after all the other boys and the police cars were long gone and Jadea remained behind talking to vendors and individuals who were working in the area. Some of them were scared to be involved with whatever business the young man had got himself involved with, but mostly they were all scared of the prison, although life in the streets and sleeping in them is another jail, just as limited as life in a cell.

Jadea could not believe Makhathini's story. He thought he was just one of the boys seeking attention. "*Why did he deny it at first*?" Ignorance is the cause of all trouble and it is directly proportional to being unreasonably obstinate. Regardless of everything, he knew that this young boy could not just disappear unless he had help in doing so! He questioned it.

Of the witnesses who might have an idea about what actually happened, two of them were certain. One was the old granny who'd seen it from her window, although her statements began with, "I am not very sure because of night blindness…"

From nowhere, the detective asked Jadea, "How did you get caught up in this? Are you not suppose to be doing something different?"

"It is a long story," replied Jadea.

Quickly the detective replied, "Every story can be short and we have all day in this car."

"What you should know is that I made a mess, so I am cleaning up after myself." After Petrus heard this, he kept quiet and stopped investigating Jadea.

Makhathini came across Jadea's mind. He felt like he could make things right with Joey through him. Joey had embarrassed him and it was hard for him to let it go. They'd all wished at one point to hang him when he messed up the operation at the beginning because they were depending on him. But Jadea had ruined his own business reputation many times.

Joey and Stanley travelled from one point to another, getting nothing. They reached the market place. This place had its own rules and George sometimes visited it, since it was the only large black market for red diamonds. Playing it hard and raw was usual behaviour for Joey, but he calmed himself in such a place. He knew one thing was certain: nobody was able to protect him from all the vicious wolves, mostly politicians, who were gaining from these people. As they went inside, two very muscular men were standing at the door. They searched for weapons. Joey carried a pistol. In that moment, he took it out and gave it to them. That was not open for discussion. They would not risk it because they knew you. They had valuables precious stones and business was business. One of them accompanied them after he'd heard the purpose for their visit. Joey was not just some freak and club banger. He walked with them to a VIP room. The room had a fish tank that separated it from the public area. The room had two men, the one African and the other one Chinese.

Last time, George had had a problem with one of the men, but when Foster and Joey arrived the man who fought with George was no longer there. They all sat on two long, leather sofas. In the club, loud music was playing but different music played in the VIP room; soft jazz and a sexy instrumental relaxation saxophone collection. The security officer who had walked them in, turned away and left them inside. This club was one of the biggest in the whole city. From time to time they would host celebrity showcases and parties.

"Hello, Zheng", Joey greeted him and shook hands with him, as they all sat down. Foster and Joey sat next to each other. Zheng was of average height and spoke fluent English. They drank whiskey. A niche market business such as this one had specific dates and schedules, so Zheng was not surprised by the visit. He'd known it was only a matter of time.

After they had exchanged greetings, Joey asked, "Have you seen my friend George lately?" He wanted to make this conversation as short as it could be. He thought that otherwise they might leave the place in body bags.

"You're quick to ask for him," Zheng replied.

Whatever he was up to, running to get there, he had to wait for some time. "So, how is business this side of the town?" Joey changed the topic but the reason he had come to this place was very clear.

Zheng noticed and replied, telling them what they needed to hear. "Yes, I did see him the other day. He was here looking for an open market." Zheng remembered the favour Joey had once done for someone he knew, so he decided to cut to the chase with him. Joey had thought it was just another roadblock, but surprisingly it turned the other way around. Despite this, he was two steps back from George's game.

After they left the club, one of his men called him, telling him that they had spotted George's moves.

"Great news!" he said. They got into the car quickly and drove away.

PETRUS WAS NOT YET AWARE of the news. He was with Jadea when they went to pick up a witness, one of the security officers at a certain bank. A manager introduced them to the man. They asked him if they could borrow him off his job. When he saw them he assumed that they were cops. What a wrong turn he had made to speak about this and he regretted it.

The Witness knew something different from everyone. That night he'd actually thought that the shots were being fired from somewhere around the bank. In his mind it was a bank robbery. To speak with the man in front of Jadea was not such a good idea because he could not be trusted. "*They might hear about another murder: that the witness was murdered.*" Many such cases have occurred. Regardless of the differences between Jadea and his cousin, he was not going to watch him go down for many years easily. It was a guarantee that he was not going to let that happen on his watch.

"Excuse me for a second." Petrus left Jadea behind and went to meet the witness to talk to him. Whatever he was going to discuss with him was between himself and the witness. Jadea was not aware that this was a witness to the case. He did not argue about it, but it seemed that the detective was not being truly honest with him. What concerned Jadea, and what did not? They chose for him.

As Petrus and the witness talked, Jadea waited for him outside the car parked along the road. Makhathini came across his mind, and for a second he thought, "*Will my misery end one day*?"

Petrus did not record anything else but he took the tape the officer brought to him. The tape was not as clear as he'd thought it would be, because this video was recorded at midnight, but he could recognise faces getting out of the car and going back into the car. With the help of the people whom Joey had brought in to help, surely they could figure out a way to zoom and scan it closely for identification.

This was his first proper breakthrough in the eyes of other cops, which was important to him since he was a people person and he always had an appetite for the spotlight. Deep inside he knew they were still very far from closing this case. When they got back, he placed the tape in his office drawer back and closed his eyes.

Chapter 11

Tanya's sister had catered for all his needs after he'd left high school for university. Soon after he'd finished high school, he'd got a girl pregnant and she had borne him a daughter. While in school, he'd had a relationship with one of the young female teachers. He was raised in a polygamous family, and his mother had been left to raise her two children by her own means. His sister had graduated with an accounting degree, and had got a good job afterwards, so ever since she had been catering for Tanya's needs. His father was a hard worker but he had his own limits and issues. It is hard however for a woman to raise a man. Tanya had lost it to meth while trying to find a perfect role model. The void of his father's love was huge and missing in his life, so he turned to drugs and made them his new home.

In the previous weeks he had visited his high school girlfriend and baby mother. She had suffered a miscarriage with their second child and all he said was that the news of miscarriage hurt him. He was having sex with any girl who showed interest in him and was probably irresponsible about the consequences of unprotected sexual activities. He wanted to have a church of kids but was never concerned about clothing and feeding them. Being *real* is what he always wanted to be but the more he hated his father, the more he turned out to be like him.

They had all gathered around and were still having the argument about selling the car. None of them had stolen a car before so this was totally a new thing and they were nervous. They left the topic unsettled, one reason being that they knew nothing about buyers.

A FATHER-SON RELATIONSHIP HAD TORN apart but that did not stop George from trying to claim his lost treasure and bring it back to where it belonged. If that meant he would be aggressive about his way of doing things, then that was it.

He received a call from Zheng. He told him, "They are like wolves crawling in every corner of the street." He then gave him the description of the man who had been with Joey, and it was exactly a match for Foster.

These were just some of the things that were stressing him, but he was in more pain because he was still in the dark about his son. He also had the drawing from an expert. He took a photo and sent it to some of the people who were quietly doing a thorough search, a search that he could not do. They told him that nothing had come up yet and it was troubling him. This was the only thing that had changed in all his plans. It dragged everything down. There is more to winning than just walking home with a trophy.

JADEA KEPT ON THINKING ABOUT Makhathini, until he decided to act on what he'd heard. At least this was the one person who had a different answer from everyone. He left alone, in his own car, to get him. They had all underestimated and insulted his intelligence. The thing he depended on most was his strong instincts in making such decisions quickly. He went back to look for Makhathini at the same place they had rounded up young boys in the previous hours. Unfortunately, when he got there not a single one of the boys hanging around was Makhathini. His eyes went back and forth everywhere. He kept on searching for them.

After about twenty minutes, he approached two men who were selling second hand jackets in the street. He first greeted them with humbleness and in an old-fashioned, respectful way, using the ordinary dialect. He asked them if they could recognise the person in the picture he had taken from his pocket. They both said they'd never seen this person before. They urged him to ask another man who worked close-by, selling cigarettes and all sorts of snacks and sweets. He had his table close to theirs. He walked over to him.

The man greeted him with a smile, "How are you, Son," he said. Jadea replied but his thoughts were elsewhere now. He'd become impatient and he felt it was a waste of time. Before he asked him about Tinashe, he saw one of the eight boys they'd rounded up in the morning. He asked him for Makhathini, and in exchange for money he agreed to show him. He knew exactly where he could find him at that time of the day. They both left and drove to the place and it was not very far away. Jadea left his car and walked on foot. He did this so that he would not scare away the birds.

Makhathini saw him approaching and he knew what was going on. He got excited and stood up to meet him half way. Makhathini's addiction mostly had been to nyaope. He would do anything to feed that addiction. Instead of giving him money, Jadea suggested buying it for him. It was a temptation he could not overcome. Makhathini thought to himself about these fancy cars and people coming to look for his friend. He wanted the same thing that had happened to Tinashe although he knew nothing about the whole story. All he wanted was to fulfil his fantasy of cars and ice. He was so eager to get out from the bottom and start dealing with the "BIG STUFF".

"Can you help me find your friend," Jadea asked nicely and convincingly, as if it were a good thing. Because of his dreams of cars and ice, Makhathini agreed because he could see what was in it for him. He never meant to betray his friend and out of his desperate thoughts persuaded himself that it was a good thing for Tinashe too.

Jadea kept on marking words up in this boy's mind. Makhathini said to Jadea, "I know one place that he might have gone, if he is not here." Jadea took him next to a close by shop and bought him new clothes and shoes, and soon after they followed Tinashe to where he had gone.

NEIL'S FRUSTRATION AFTER HE'D HIDDEN the gun abused his thoughts. He wanted that car for himself. They'd spent the whole day having fun, which meant drinking and smoking with their crew and with clueless woman who gave them more than just their company. That is what life meant to them. After all, the commercials had set the scene and had done a good job in that. Mostly after smoking and still drinking, they got on their phones, taking photos and uploading for likes and comments.

Tinashe was playing games on Neil's laptop because Tanya had sold most of his gadgets to feed his crack addiction. His sister spoiled him and she had given him her cell phone after he had sold his for drugs. It was another pain, but she endured, thinking he was going to stop using the drugs, and he had always denied the fact that he was an addict.

Neil wondered to himself, *Why am I sticking around these crack addicts*, so bit by bit he packed his clothes and was getting ready to leave with the car. He planned to use the gun on whomever might try to stop him.

He wanted more space to pack his things. He asked the other two if they would go and buy a bucket of food. After all, they were all hungry and they could use a good meal. Reverse psychology. They were too lazy to go and buy food. But cleaning the place was more painful than that, so he suggested to them that they go and leave him behind to round up everything. He added that he knew a person who had an idea about a place where they bought stolen cars. Eventually they fell for it and he remained behind, packing what he could.

DETECTIVE MDUDUZI LOCKED HIS OFFICE doors and watched the footage repeatedly. He showed it to his trustworthy officers and the investigation kept on going. He reported the car, and its number plate. He'd only assumed that it was the car that they had used as a get-away car.

The picture became clearer and it was much easier to recognise that the picture did not have George in it. The bags were carried by the young man, probably Tinashe. Foster was the other man. They questioned themselves twice about the minions, whether they did all the killing.

FOSTER HEARD ABOUT THE CAR and he ran down to the warehouse to look for it. He got there and he was left amazed. He'd had no idea that it was gone and that scared him the most. He suspected George. He felt insecure about this. Now someone had something to use against him. If it were not George, then it was just a coincidence.

He decided to keep quiet about it. The trouble was left for the one who was going to be caught with it.

NEIL KEPT ON PACKING HIS clothes and some shoes that did not belong to him that he had borrowed from some of his friends. As fast as possible, he gathered up everything around him. When they came back they would find him gone. He took the money they had left him with. He took the bag and threw it on the back seat of the car they had stolen.

Neil thought about how everybody back home was going to be startled by him. The car would be a sign of prosperity among his old friends who lived back at his hometown. Most of them were alcoholics and, if not, then successful drug dealers. Lately he had been struggling with rent payments. None of his relatives were looking out for him. This was an act of desperation. He carried his bag downstairs quickly.

When Tinashe and Tanya came back from a supermarket close by, something did not add up. The house was just too clean and clear. Tinashe stood by the window and when he saw a flash of the car he felt the rapture of menace. He ran downstairs, followed by Tanya who also had assumed something was wrong. The security guards delayed them and Tinashe had lost sight of the car when he got out, but his hopes to find it were still high. Where they had parked, it definitely was now just an empty space. Neil had played them for fools.

Both of them felt like they had lost track of time and it was simply déjà vu again. He blamed himself for trusting a cocaine and cat addict. This was just more bad luck. He did not know that even more bad luck was on its way because Jadea and Makhathini were coming for him.

FOSTER HAD NOT EXPECTED ANY of this to happen so quickly but suddenly it did happen, and to keep him away from all the coming and never-ending problems was a nightmare. He had become a witness of a horror world. He only hoped to get out of this with a clean sheet and go back to his old life. This happens when people are not careful about what they wish for. When you keep on travelling via a difficult road, it is going to become difficult for you to come back.

SOON AFTER JOEY'S UNIT GOT hold of George, they agreed to meet up with him at a certain place and he gave them terms and conditions of the meeting. These were trouble men. He specified that they should not bring friends of friends, but he was telling a deaf man a story. George told them he wanted to apologize sincerely to Foster for shooting him.

Jadea had called him telling him about all the places he could find the young man. They both agreed that Tinashe had hidden himself from everyone. Zheng kept on giving George the heads up whenever changes occurred. These games and players would piss on each other's heads and claim that it was rain.

George left his apartment with his gun behind his back. Detective Mduduzi left the station with other police officers for an arrest. They were all set to apprehend him. They tried to keep the arrest confidential but the word got out as always. Joey also took some men from his unit. Foster and Jadea were not invited to this party.

Foster remembered Dr. Choo, who'd fixed his shoulder socket. He was not just any doctor, but he spent time at hospitals treating patients and he kept his political life decent. Foster was still curious about everything that was written down in his case, and he was kept in the darkness about it. This was a way of threatening him from time to time whenever he slipped up.

Choo was aware of the security officer who'd died during the robbery. Before he'd lost consciousness he must have said something. Choo had connections countrywide. He had a previous history of being involved in the forefront of freedom struggles against all the kinds of segregation that were happening in the world in the 1980s, especially in Africa.

Neil had found what he'd always wanted; he was "balling" in his new car, non-stop. Notorious people are the ones who usually use such cars. Tinashe ran upstairs to tell this to Tanya. He banged the door, breathing hard and Tanya thought "*What a joke*". This was just news that mattered, and not because Tanya's eyes had almost shed tears when he'd found out that his good sneakers were gone.

He felt a moment of depression. It was outrageous how angry he was. If Neil had been close-by, they would have fought to the death. He was high and he felt the lowness of it. They had all sorts of bogus talk but it was not helping. Again, and as usual, they sought comfort in marijuana for relief. They ate the food they had brought from the supermarket.

George had rented a warehouse with cash, and he stood in the midst of it. Joey walked in alone. Intriguing and true it was. When they met at first hand, you would almost think they were friends. The silence broke. "Do you want to take it there?" Joey asked. They were both determined; perseverance and persistence made them alike.

"Years have passed without seeing your face. Actually, you have not changed at all," George replied. "Only a few months ago we talked on the phone," he added.

Happy conversation stopped chop-chop. It was not a comedy show. Joey blamed George for bringing troubles to his door step. "Realise how every peace of mind we ever had was short-lived, ephemeral."

George referred to the people Joey was still getting orders from, for Joey had sworn to stay loyal to his grave. Joey's loyalty was paid back by an unlimited number of resources.

"If you want the bag, first bring my son," George said.

"At least meet me half way," Joey replied.

It was impossible in the eyes of George to give in, but he suggested that they end this in a civilised and professional way. Joey then told him that he had no other options but to arrest him. Without argument, George agreed to the arrest. The time he had been falsely accused and had spent about one hundred and seventy days in solitary confinement was nothing to the pain of betrayal. However, George was not innocent of the new murder charges.

All of a sudden he was surrounded by different men approaching him from all sides, including Petrus Mduduzi. He walked out of the warehouse handcuffed. They had all expected him to put up a fight but they did not question his intention. After all, he had spent time running away from each one of them. He was in the back of the car as they drove to the station. It was a thirty-minute drive due to road traffic.

They avoided questioning him and even a simple conversation was hard. He knew they had not won but for starters he was in their hands to play with. Joey sat in the front with his gun on his thigh, just in case of any fun and games. They were stuck in a situation where thirty minutes seemed like two days.

Detective Mduduzi was behind them in his car.

George asked, "So who sent you this time, Joey?"

"You only heard a rumour that you might have a son and you believed it. How desperate are you for a child? Your thoughts are sailing on the same ship." George kept quiet in the face of this teasing. Joey said, "Now you are biting the hand that feeds you. This is embarrassing of you, George." When Joey started talking, he took over the whole conversation and started preaching. "You have demolished the image you took time to build and all your loyal disciples are left destitute. The so-called son that you have mentioned earlier, you barbarously used him as bait for your prey. You went overboard, as usual."

George mentioned about child abuse in the company they both once worked for, although Joey was still operative in it. Mostly nobles had set up the whole structure for profit making. Others, especially low lifes, played robots who knew not what they were doing. They had always kept themselves at the top with the others, not realising their lives had been a part of a whole plot. When George was awakened and had climbed out of the icebox, they all had a problem because he was starting to take from them in large amounts. All those who were with him in decision making left him to die lonely. They reached a decision that placed his head on a bounty.

Joey was quick to speak, and fast to anger, and lastly slow to listen.

They got him to the station and used a back door to one of the single cells. Back in the day, many people died in those cells after being brutally tortured. One of the reasons they used that door was in order to not attract attention to whom they had brought in. Detective Mduduzi had promised the news team something, but Joey was not to entertain them.

George kept on talking to Joey. "You know how much these kids yearn for the glamorous fruit they do not have, and they idolise the celebrities that do. It is a shame that they are willing to do anything crazy for it, instead of going to school."

Joey replied to him, "It is not you who should decide which road they are willing to take and you will not change their own foolishness. George, my old friend, you cannot change the whole world. Instead, it changes you."

They left him inside a cell.

JADEA WAS IN HIS CAR and, with the help of Makhathini, his enthusiasm was once again renewed. They wanted to get there fast but, because of it, it seemed like it was rather a journey to heaven. Most of what they said to each other did not go well and they could relate to nothing besides the marijuana they smoked all the way. Makhathini kept on selling himself to Jadea, telling him all kinds of stuff he could do for him. Clearly he was begging for a chance to a better life.

"Favour for a favour, my friend," Jadea replied to him, and promised him all kinds of flash lights, cameras and action.

After Makhathini heard this, he could see himself on top of all the billboard charts. He felt awakened by it. Living in the streets had made him fade away; he was ready, even at the expense of losing his soul, to get out of it.

LATER THAT SAME EVENING, AN officer was found unconscious in the jail. You would have thought he'd tripped and fallen, or that something had been used to hit his head very hard. George had struck him with a rod, and someone had intentionally given him that rod. It was a very crucial blow.

Two officers had been given the responsibility of keeping a very close eye as Joey and Detective Mduduzi sorted out the papers to transfer him to a private facility. Those officers tried, but suddenly he'd started begging for water, acting up as if he were dying of thirst; he was annoying them unpleasantly. One left to grab a jar and George started choking as if he had consumed some poison. Without any knowledge, the second young officer wanted to check and he opened the cell.

George had not had any plans to stay inside for long, so he found his way out quickly. His mission was to grab all the information in the evidence room that had his name on the cover. He removed the clothes he was wearing and took one of the officer's and he walked, looking down to avoid cameras. It was the right moment for any unexpected escape such as this one. Everyone had relaxed in their comfort zone.

Joey was still in the station at that time. Three of them were having a discussion to allow him to take George with him. Joey, Detective Mduduzi and the Chief Colonel were having this discussion. George walked unnoticed to the evidence room. He asked for the papers, pretending that he was a new transfer, since everybody was aware of this operation. He walked like an officer and roared like an officer, and he did not look nervous even once. He saw the file number and diligently asked for it. He signed off the documents then started reading them. They would not allow him to take the papers away, and so he made a plan. As soon as the evidence was in his hands, he replaced the old papers with plain white sheets from a nearby photocopy machine so they did not notice anything. He was still curious about what was in Detectives Mduduzi's office. When it comes to old tactics, he was surely ancient with these tricks.

MAKHATHINI KNEW TANYA'S FLAT. JADEA parked the car outside. He went to the security desk for ID checking but he did not only show them his ID. He provided a fake police ID card too. He took out Tinashe's picture and pressed it against the glass. The security officer checked. For a moment he was confused and asked himself why this police officer was looking for the young man.

Jadea took Makhathini with him. They went to the room registered to Neil Hadebe and Tanya. Recognising Tanya was easy because of his brownish dreadlocks that his sister kept on telling him to cut off.

Joey noticed another car outside and he thought it looked familiar. A traffic police officer had pulled it alongside the pavement that was opposite the police station. The driver was driving slowly to attract attention, surely. The car looked much like Foster's, but the person who was standing next to it was not Foster. He thought to have a closer look at it, but then he noticed unusual movement. All the officers were running into the station. The word was out and the alarm was making a noise.

He suspected only one thing: his former friend had found a way out of the cell. He ignored the car and turned to the situation at hand. "What happened," he called out, but no one was there to answer all his questions, so he grabbed another officer with a strong grip and asked him.

"A prisoner who was recently brought in, escaped," the officer replied.

"How could you let this happen?" he furiously asked, but no one answered him. The officer was long gone. He was losing time.

George was in the garage with paper files in his hand and the keys of a car that was in the garage for him. This had been a well-planned mission right from the start, but now he had clearly become a fugitive.

Joey had lost his prisoner on his watch. He was angry at himself and especially at everyone who had been delaying in processing the papers for him to put George in a confined area with proper watch and security.

JADEA WALKED INTO THE ROOM and found Tinashe and Tanya asleep, as they had drunk themselves out. His hand was on his belt, to get his gun quickly if required. He wanted to threaten Tinashe with it,

Makhathini stayed outside the door. Before Jadea had gone inside, he had suggested that Makhathini should go back to the car. This scared him. Whatever was happening was so bad it could hurt his friend in the process.

Slowly, Jadea went and sat next to Tinashe and started waking him up, but he was too intoxicated to respond immediately. When he woke up after a few minutes and noticed who was sitting next him, he pretended that he was dreaming but the sudden coldness he felt was real. For Tanya, with all the drugs he had consumed, waking up was for the next day.

Nicely, Jadea asked Tinashe if they could leave the place in one piece, before any further collateral damage happened. He only left quietly because the gun petrified him by just looking at it. Since its invention, it only had one purpose and he knew it clearly.

Once they had stepped outside, Jadea said, “I tried to play nice, but you took advantage”.

Tinashe had, however, lost most of his fears of these men. He replied to him, “Why am I so special to you, that you could not let it go.” Good music had stopped playing for the young man. He was back in the same situation as before. He’d thought that once he had escaped, he had a new hope for tomorrow. Silently they walked together. He thought of himself as less important, just like others, and that made him stand by himself firmly.

Jadea promised to give him a present on the back of his skull if he even thought of running away for a second. When Tinashe saw Makhathini, it was not a big surprise but disappointing. Makhathini, however, was happy to see his buddy.

Makhathini’s turning point in his life was when he became an addict of nyaope. He was introduced to it through marijuana. Since the day that someone had given him a joint with it in, he never wanted again to smoke anything different from that.

He had drawn Jadea to Tinashe without thinking of the consequences. All he’d wanted was to give his friend a better opportunity and it was not an act of betrayal. “Looking out for each other, even through dark times,” they’d pledged this code. Tinashe was furious but he was concerned about how doomed his friend’s mind was.

The conversation between Joey and the police officers was not an easy one. Now they all agreed that their cells were no longer fit to contain George if they captured him again. Next time he stood no chance of escaping that easily. Their reputation had been ruined so badly and the media would be uncomplimentary the following morning. The number of officers and other private investigators increased rapidly.

Nobody had informed Foster about the progress that had been made. However, he received a call from Joey Morish. On the phone, Joey mentioned only pieces of the story and left Stanley hooked on it. What Joey did not mention was Foster's car, although he was eager to know what had happened to it. He only had a small idea about how Foster might have played them for fools and helped George out, since they both could not be trusted at this moment. It was convincing enough to point a finger at him right away.

In the car, George received a message from Jadea. He had sent George a photo message. The image he sent was that of Tinashe. He wanted to convince him, if he should be happy about the news, but it was going from bad to worse and a new situation had arisen. Politics is like Tetris and every block should go exactly where it is required.

The first demand that came along with the message was, "If you would like to see your boy again, bring me the head of Morish." Jadea's hatred for Morish was outrageous. He'd let it mature inside of him. Nothing was more precious to him than revenge.

George, for and instant, thought of going back. "*No way. It is surely a lion's den.*" He understood that the first enemy is yourself, followed by your best friend whose enemies are as much as yours and, lastly, the one true enemy whose name is never known.

Jadea's motive for joining George was not money based at all and that made him more dangerous. Now he had all the power to complete the threesome. The end seemed near, but time keeps on going and waiting for the few left to repent. Jadea's business and its ways were barely supported by any form of ethics and no form of legitimacy. Revenge made him incompetent in just a few days.

The love George had for the young boy confused his mind and filled it with arguments. The bad feeling he felt for abandoning him once, moved his deepest love closer.

A SHORT TIME AFTER JADEA had left with Tinashe, Neil came rushing in and woke Tanya up. He had come back to look for Tinashe, and he noticed that the young man was no longer around.

Even though the boys thought that they had searched Foster's car thoroughly, a phone had been left hidden somewhere inside the car and it belonged to none of them. When Neil had run away with the car, Foster had repeatedly called that phone. After a while, Neil had stopped and found the phone, and when it rang again he had answered it. Neil had been promised death if he did not go back to Tinashe and Tanya. Foster had told him that the car did not matter, but that the boy was worth more than any other asset. So Neil had driven back.

At that time, Jadea was driving in the dark. He stopped at a petrol station. There, he told Makhathini to get out of the car. He threatened him using his gun, so he quickly jumped out of the car. He looked for Tinashe's help but he never found it. He was nervous and clueless of what had just happened to him. Jadea scared him away and Makhathini almost peed in his pants.

After this, Jadea turned to Tinashe and told him, "You and I still have unfinished business, my brother. If your father does not keep to the new agreement that we made, it is unfortunate for you because I would be forced to bury your head six feet down. No more games, all right!"

Makhathini ran for his life as fast as he could. He did not turn around to see if his friend was okay. Jadea had played him like solitaire. He did not bother to look back to see if he was being followed, and so he ran into the woods and hid behind a shrub.

Jadea received a call from Foster on the driveway, and he answered it, looking into the eyes of Tinashe so that he would not play any games with him.

"Where are you? We need to meet immediately. Something has come up," Foster said.

"What is it," Jadea replied and added, "I am far away". Foster gave him a brief résumé of what had happened at the police station. He was surprised when he heard the news. Foster told him they could hook up later, after Jadea had travelled back. From that call he also understood one thing: the rivalry between Joey and George was very lucrative. Jadea was running away from making his hands dirty but he wanted George's dirty hands to do it.

George pulled the car alongside the road after he was very far from his hunters, to think about all of this, and for some breathing space. He was determined to pull Morish into the hell pit with him. His destination changed. He was now going back to the station. He went on to dial Joey's private number. Joey was not expecting such a caller.

"I have a deal to cut with you. Let us again meet in person and this time bring nobody with you – and when I say nobody, I mean it or else I will disappear and go to Europe forever until your death."

"Do not take chances with me, if you have everything you want, then why would you need a deal to settle for less," Joey replied to George. After this, he was surely convinced that George might not be joking and it seemed as if this conversation was the last one.

George dropped the call. Now he was in the corner of an alliance. People usually join forces with a better devil to destroy the worse one and so that they could both have a piece of him. When this successfully happens, they turn against each other in the end because of greed. A devil is a devil, not good or better, because the result is usually the same. A dance with him might last forever.

George made more calls to different friends to back up the situation. Joey felt he also had it under control, but the pressure gave him all sorts of frustrations. He asked Detective Mduduzi for help in this and told him he was no longer trusting anybody, including Mbali. Apparently, Detective Mduduzi gave up the will to spend time with his family and turned to his job with undivided attention.

Foster got to the station with high expectations that everyone would be running around. However, everything seemed normal and even calmer than in the days before.

Joey and George came to an agreement and made arrangements for a new meeting. Petrus and Joey made sure that the alliance would be in their favour and as easy as birds picking and eating bread crumbs. Joey never did forget that their reputation had been broken into pieces by this jailbird. Right at that moment, reputation did not matter, but those diamonds were worth something. If it was about status, George was left without any. After he'd spent all those years behind bars, all his mercenary work was flushed down the drain. Crime does not pay, no matter how big it might be. It will hurt you and it is just a matter of time.

Elsewhere, the news of the escape reached the wrong ears. Many doubted and anonymous decisions were made. The question was whether Sergeant Joey could handle this case better than he had already done. They needed someone with more strength and knowledge than Joey had. The people who were affected by all these difficulties reached him and left a message on his phone. They scheduled a meeting with him but it quickly turned out that the appointment collided with the one George wanted. The people who hired him were scarier than George or anything he was doing for the moment. They never took "no" for an answer. His power was zero when compared to them. Shareholders were serpents and wolves purposely placed in power.

Joey knew how bad the situation had turned out to be. He left Petrus to handle the search for George. Petrus adopted "shock and awe", a military mantra itself; a military term, that seeks to neutralise the enemy and then destroying him complete.

Foster went to the police station very angry. Somebody had stolen his car and he was filing a case about it. Someone was watching all these people very closely. Somebody had had enough guts to snatch it away silently. Two officers left with him to go and check if what he was saying was for real, and it checked out.

"Detective, you are going with these two men to help you if there are any troubles," Morish said to Petrus, appointing two of his men as if he had another choice. From the seven of them, Foster left and Joey went with the other two.

In the boot of Jadea's car, Tinashe's hands and feet were tied with a rope. He could sleep but dreams were impossible at that time. Jadea was driving in the middle of a road. His eyes were set on the rear view mirror. A car kept on following him and raised his suspicions. As he increased the speed, the car behind him increased its speed, but after a while it overtook him and switched off its headlights. The driver was playing with him. More than once he switched them on and off. After about half a kilometre, the car pulled over to the side of the road.

Jadea noticed that the car belonged to Foster and felt relaxed about it. His only thought was, "*How did he get here?*" He pulled his car behind it. He walked over to the car with a gun in his hand. He looked over to see who was in the car, but the darkness swallowed the driver up.

Neil had come back at the right time. After seeing that Tinashe had gone, he and Tanya had run down the stairs again and had seen Jadea forcing Tinashe to walk to his car. After that, they followed him all the way. When Jadea approached the car, a bullet was fired and it hit his thigh. He dropped his gun. "Oh, not again," he said. Neil came from behind him and took Jadea by total surprise.

Jadea hid himself behind a tree, going into the woods close by, paralysed by fear for his life. They ran up to look for him everywhere but he was nowhere to be seen. Jadea's gun lay next to their vehicle.

They looked for Tinashe in the car but were disappointed. They took the car with them and regretted only leaving Jadea alive. You reap what you sow and men do not forgive.

The two cars turned around, finding their way back. The two of them thought that maybe Tinashe had been murdered and his body thrown away in the woods. Moreover, they figured out that going to the same apartment, even with the security of two guns, was no longer safe. Many people were now fully aware of the place and Makhathini was always available to bring them for tours.

Unexpectedly, these two students started making things happen for themselves. Tanya drove away followed by Neil in Jadea's car. A phone that was on the dashboard started to ring a few minutes later. Neil took it and threw it out of the car.

Lying in the boot, Tinashe's feeling of coming home was all gone and torn into pieces.

Chapter 12

Detective Mduduzi went to another police station to check himself in. It was anyway the closest to the place Joey had arranged a meeting with George. He was to meet George secretly and re-discuss the predicaments that recently had been the talk of the town. He did not know what to expect from this meeting. One thing was certain and that was he'd never leave his gun behind. Without any further delays he went up to meet up with George.

George had become agitated because he kept on trying to reach out to Jadea. Another thing that was unpleasant in his sight was surprises. He also went to his scheduled meeting but this time he was not going to let them arrest him just for fun. Anything that was going to happen, the detective would sweep under the carpet. The night had set whatever the night had planned for them, but would probably leave no witnesses.

FOURTH DAY

Early the next morning it was the fourth day of confusion about what was happening around them. Larger problems were arising and the table was still full of them. Joey came back that morning looking for updates on what to do. His focus had however changed. Now what he was looking forward to doing was laying the case to rest by leaving the person who started all this with a bullet in his skull. That was the only way to silence him. More things were set on the line, which meant property, assets and names of big players. If the truth was to be set out in broad daylight, it would be the downfall and humiliation of many. The time for meetings and negotiations was finally over.

Not everyone was going to agree to this method, but it was not open for discussion. Specific information held in a flash drive George had taken was too valuable to be in his hands. This was the same type of information another detective had lost his life over, about seven years ago. George was persistent about getting it out there. When this detective accepted to work with him, it was too heavy for his shoulders and he could not hold the weight. He was brutally violated at the hands of these men. The exchange George had asked from the detective was information that was going to help him locate his son.

George carried the grievance and desperations of justice of the other side, and yet he felt locked away in a vault. His focus to loot out Detective Mduduzi for chitchat successfully worked. His idea was to remove any interruptions, especially those who knew about his life before; he wanted to talk to Petrus in private. George only saw a snitch whenever he looked at Joey. Joey came back with a convoy and they acted late because the revelation had already started.

Two hours after Jadea got shot, Tanya and Neil went back and left their place without notice. They packed the rest of their stuff, which was not a lot anyway. They only assumed he was following after them.

"This does not look good," said Tanya.

"Why? Are you scared!" Neil exclaimed.

They left all the goods at a close-by small warehouse with cheap rental. Four hours had passed when they went to look for something to turn up. "All of a sudden we have two different cars and yet neither of us actually has a driver's licence," Tanya said. In the background music was playing very loudly so that they could barely hear each other talking and cigarette were scattered all over. Tanya wanted to ask him where the gun Neil had used to shoot Jadea had come from, but he was too worried about other things to be bothered with it. They both started joking around that they had got two guns on the same day. They shared these two guns between themselves.

Later, Neil opened the boot and found Tinashe inside, sleeping. They all got excited. An old thesis was reformed with the profound understanding of how deeply they were involved in this.

Tinashe angrily punched Neil after he got out of the car. He had a major reason, and the reason came from being disappointed after seeing him driving away with what he had worked for.

They found more money hidden under the seat of Jadea's car; the same money George had given Jadea to find his son for him. Tanya screamed while they were still searching for more things. "This is a lot of money."

Tinashe felt the happiest moment he ever had in his life, looking at freedom. Whatever he was holding against these two, he thanked them for getting him out of grave danger. Neil following Jadea, that he had stolen the car in the first place, and other series of events that followed, seemed like they were destined to happen. He told them what had happened and what had got him in the ropes, and in the boot of the car. He had been asking so many questions that Jadea had got fed up by them and had thrown him into the boot.

From this point onwards, Tinashe knew that these two had put down and risked their lives just to save him. It gave him a sense of self-belief, family and importance. He loved standing with his new brothers. His thoughts were motivated by getting money and making more money.

"This is what Jadea told me, when I asked a question about why I was important to him. He mentioned that my father, who I've recently run into and who tried to pull a trigger on me, has placed money on me, and I will never trust him at all. The man tried to kill me once and he could try it again. He is not my father, for anytime soon. We have money to make a strong plan against him. Let us try it. We have half of it on the silver plate and Foster knows," Tinashe said.

ALL PETRUS WAS THINKING WAS arrogance within him and how proud he was that he was about to bring in one of the biggest crime bosses. This time the man was going down forever. This was a lifetime achievement. Not only would it make his name, but he could start that security company he'd always wanted.

FOSTER WAS OUT EARLY, FOR the scene and a call from Jadea had changed his mood for the whole morning. Jadea had told him that a couple of amateurs had stolen his car and he blamed it on Foster, insisting that they had used a car just like Foster's and that had confused him about the whole situation. He kept on insisting that in a way Foster was the mastermind of this incident. Family blood was off limits from the start.

Foster said that this anger was due to the cocaine Jadea was constantly taking. Foster suggested that, instead of sprinkling family blood on the altar, he should find an animal and slaughter that instead.

JOEY KEPT ON MOTIVATING OTHERS. "We spot him and bury him, then we can all go back to our families."

THE THREE TROUBLEMAKERS WERE LOOKING forward to being back in the City of Gold, leaving the small valley for a city with major hunters. They wanted to get rid of the two cars before trouble from the police started knocking on their doors. The fact was that they had been lucky so far, and nothing was ever scarier or more funny than this.

At about eight o'clock in the morning, a truce was made and they were able to exchange two illegal cars in return for one legal one, with money on top of it. They took a decent and dependable vehicle with tinted windows. They gassed up and sped off. The three militant and impatient youths had one goal in common: to get rich or die trying.

FOSTER WAS QUIET FOR A time after he realised there was just too much beef being slaughtered at his table. His life was falling apart. Jadea was just adding more salt while a lion was eating Foster.

Jadea wondered why he'd got involved in all of this. He'd lost the very thing that was important to him and now they had both lost their cars on the same day. Walking like a penguin because of the bullet stuck in his leg, he tried to stop passing cars but people just could not afford the risk at that hour. Many people who have been hi-jacked before would be familiar with the methods: you see an man with a limp standing by the road side looking for transport. Out of a good heart you stop to find out that his colleagues suddenly show up with AK 47s, busting knee caps and hitting your head and doing you harm for money.

JOEY HAD BECOME UNSETTLED SINCE the meeting the night before. His actions were paranoid, even towards Detective Mduduzi, and he was easily disturbed. He questioned how George had escaped from this very secure place and if the station commander had anything to do with it. After being nagged repeatedly with questions of the meeting, Petrus kept on replying with the same answer. He could not tell him the whole truth because so much was offered and his career was about to explode in the blink of an eye, like the coming of Christ. Petrus knew if he could get this done in time, surely he was walking away from this with a bag of money and fame. All Petrus had ever wanted was to be more than just a police officer; he wanted to be respected above anything else.

GEORGE OPENED HIS EYES, WATCHING a bunch of hypocrites with skeletons in their eyes. He had felt used and humiliated for his entire life, making others big while remaining at the bottom, thinking that is exactly where he belonged. Outrageous tycoons and conmen who were certified tyrants ruled over him.

TINASHE AND HIS FRIENDS COULD argue vehemently as always over matters of the matrix, and always they kept themselves heavily medicated. The arguments pertaining to life were very rare; mostly it was based on commercial hip-hop music. They found such music inspiring, like never before, yet they forgot it is only entertainment. They'd promised each other not to consume any drugs but it turned out to be a very short-lived promised. Neil was confident enough that these drugs were making him fearless. Tinashe had promised his friends that if they would treat him with respect and as an equal despite his age, he was truly going to treat them well too and he swore this by his tongue and by his mother's grave.

JOEY WENT TO GET A warrant. He forced Detective Mduduzi into a corner to get this right. A young police officer he monitored from time to time knew more about the missing evidence but it was not of concern at this point.

George had told the detective to smell those around him, so he looked at his own Colonel. He noticed how his boss' career was making progress because he was very favoured. "*But why*?" he thought. He made deals with high profile criminals until they were above the law. From time to time, just to keep the work going, these criminals gave up some of their mates. They would not even reach the police station and all that was ever heard was that, "*They were shot dead in a gunfight*". The same thing had been attempted on George's life. In this way, they avoided witnesses. If this failed, another person would face false allegations from nowhere, just to remove him from the position he held so that he could be replaced with a puppet. Business continued as usual: the rich got richer and the poor got poorer.

George knew many corrupt individuals and he had some evidence against these business owners and politicians, so he had given Petrus about a quarter of the names of such people and the names were accompanied by evidence to prove it. Until they met again, he would be out of the picture and could do his own thing. Otherwise, he knew sticking around in a battleground was an invitation to the graveyard.

Detective Mduduzi initiated his meeting as if he were helping Joey. Long ago he had sold him out for a greater good. Friends change. When new friends appear, you can never accept the same love from an old friend because a lot has happened on the way, but an old friend is still a friend and, when forgiven, that friend is won back and never an enemy again. Some do not understand it. Even the simplest story of love will never come out as you have imagined. Joey played a hero when his closet was full of skeletons. Physical ageing is inevitable but when hatred sets out, it remains young, powerful and energetic.

THE DRIVE TOOK ALMOST THREE hours. It was about eleven in the morning. Tinashe sat in the back seat; Tanya and Neil were in the front seats. On the way, because of speed and loud noise, the traffic police stopped them. Surprisingly, when he was asked for it Neil took out a driver's license that belonged to his brother and gave it to the cop. Neil also gave him money and, just like that, he came back to the car and drove away like nothing had happened. He had just run into hustlers in uniforms.

"NOTHING HAS COME UP YET." Joey heard this, impatient and sweating as the clock was ticking. His focus was on the monitors. They had set up a smart surveillance system they'd brought from China to upgrade the old system.

JADEA WAS LUCKY THAT THE police noticed him and took him to the hospital. When they asked for the whole truth, he forgot to mention the part where he had kidnapped someone. He exaggerated about assaults and bullets shot from robbers, and he reported his car missing. He received a police clearance for hospitals to treat him well. His leg was treated and he was guaranteed safety. The bullet that came out of his leg was from the gun Foster had bought; he'd once played with the same gun, checking if it was loaded from time to time. Now, however, he was pissed off.

DETECTIVE MDUDUZI WAS BUSY ELSEWHERE asking questions about his Colonel's whereabouts. His questioning was very annoying. The Colonel was busy sorting their way out of this. He was putting all the information together, so that he would know what to say to the newspapers and authorities above him.

DURING THIS HOUR, FOSTER HUMBLED himself and prayed.

It is all You, my Lord. I have walked in separate ways. Please let this one not be my last.

Forgive me, my Father, and I thank You for helping me through rough patches of this life of mine.

Just a thought and a smile gives me courage and hope for a better tomorrow.

My curse is that I have failed to give up my lust for money. I cannot throw these precious stones away in the water.

I thank You for walking with me, Father. Amen.

After this prayer, he took his gun, forcing his injured hand to work when needed.

TINASHE AND HIS FRIENDS WENT to a hotel and visited some of the shops that surrounded it, upgrading their style so that they could look like multi-millionaire young people.

They went into a mall to buy extravagant designer clothes. That the world is yours looked real, especially after loading up with a few Coronas and indulging habits that very few condone. Spending on what they could, Neil had a bed of drugs he wanted most, and Tanya craved much for it; as is well known, all drug addicts will do anything for few grams.

Jadea was left with a hanging idea of what he thought was happening with these boys. Surely they must have been enjoying the money and cocaine that was in the car.

Tinashe bought a new phone to call George and this he did secretly. He went into a room where he was alone and he dialled George's number. The call went through.

"Hello, who is this?" George asked.

"Tinashe," he replied quickly.

George got off his seat and stood up. For the past days, he'd prayed to receive such a call. "Tinashe!" he exclaimed and then asked, afraid that someone might be playing a joke on him, "Where are you right now?"

Before Tinashe had a chance to reply, George apologized sincerely about how badly things had gone the last time they met.

Tinashe only said, "I am coming to see you the day after tomorrow".

George insisted on coming to get him because he was not safe out there, but the reply silenced him. "I have been living in these streets, begging for food my entire life so what can you tell me about danger? I live and eat danger every day."

George was eager to make up for the lost time in their lives.

FOSTER'S RELATIONSHIP WITH TANYA HAD started when Foster had a fling with Tanya's sister – but love does not flourish when commitment lacks, and that had been short lived. However, Foster had left Tanya owing him a favour after Tanya had got himself involved with a drug pusher's money. Foster had kept on telling him to do things to repay the debt, but there was never an end to it until Foster had paid it. Tanya's sister never heard about any of this, but Tanya knew his debt to Foster would come back hard, sometime later in life, and this was that moment. They knew he was a very difficult man. He injected fear into them and stepped aside to let it grow. Now they listened to his instruction on the phone. When they agreed to work for him, their bills were no longer a problem.

In a conversation that many wanted to eavesdrop on, Detective Mduduzi was furious when confronting his boss, before making further investigation into those who were above him. Ego strengthened him; he failed to see the log in his eye but recognised that needle in another's eye.

"Do you know that this will wrap most of us, including you, and lives here are in dangerous positions now," the Colonel argued with Petrus.

"But you knew that this was going to happen to him and you let them set fire and watched him burn in a furnace," he replied, talking about the lost officer he'd replaced.

"It is unfortunate for you that former national police Colonel General Siyabongille has backed down. Despite the fact that he is facing an investigation by the Independent Police Investigation Directorate – IPID – he always gets out of this clean." The Colonel started telling him new private secrets.

"So are you willing to bet your whole family's lives and those of your relatives based on what George calls the truth? It is death, that is what it is. Leave this rubbish before it determines your destiny. George is full of filthy lies told just to achieve what he wants most, probably control," the Colonel exaggerated harshly. "My worst mistake was letting you handle this case. No matter who you send after the former colonel, they will only take disciplinary action against Siya, and he has already been cleared in a corruption report for the past three months. He will do anything to stop you from dragging his name through the mud for that old case."

He cleared his throat and drank a glass of water with a lemon slice.

He added, "The IPID have a questionable way of doing things and since it is mostly forensic investigations, someone will try to stop it. You are a stubborn man, you will definitely continue with this after what I have just said to you. What you might do to help yourself is join a campaign to discredit him and other former senior officials, but be warned that all these people have strong powers and support. They will have your family's heads delivered to you in a cooler box. You have seen how evidence disappears easily and now think about everything you have built here! You are about to lose it and I am warning you again: beware!"

Petrus stood there as if he were deaf to all this.

"I do not have any problem with the investigation and you can conduct it in the way you see fit. Maybe if you find the underlying cause of this, we would all get answers that I personally have feared to ask for. If you need help, call me any time," the Colonel said.

Then there was a call on his landline. "Can you please excuse me! I need to take this call very quickly."

Petrus opened the door and left, yet he was not convinced enough. Arrogance plus ignorance is equal to a complete disaster. He thought, "*This is not about scrutinising a career but to boost it by courage. George has enough evidence to incriminate Siya for many charges such as bribery, fraud and murder*."

The detective sat in his office thinking about why his own boss was defensive, as if he had a burden to carry on his back. Perhaps he was deeper in than the other boys were. *These men are supposed to be behind bars, yet they live and eat freely.*

He called George soon after. "Give me one name, George, that I can verify with, before I risk my life for this," he asked on the phone, hoping to get a chance to do some proper detective work.

George replied to him, "Go to Club SF and ask for Zheng, who will confirm everything. Do not think for a second that he is a snitch or otherwise he will condemn you out of his presence quickly," he urged. “Pollution is bad for the environment. Just be nice,” he urged again.

Meanwhile, George was occupied by his plans to go to the bank that had kept his belongings safely. What he had in mind was to collect his things and get ready to go away with the young boy. He wanted to buy new clothes for him and other things. The last time he could not stand the odour of the child, as if it really mattered. He didn’t know Tinashe’s size but made his best estimates. He had already started living the hardships of a father. His new character was admirable in some ways. He was tender-hearted and simple, despite the greediness that had brought him to his current situation. The addiction to his status was like that of Nyaope powder mixed with water in a syringe, called *bluetooth*. Addicts shared it like food, killing themselves.

Tinashe was familiar with it. Although he had not reached that stage of addiction yet, he was getting there. A few hours before the robbery of the bags, he had taken some to wash away the fear for he had never done anything like that for wealth before. When they had been going to the warehouse, his thoughts were only about running away with whatever was in the bags. It was Foster who’d convinced him not to. They had sent him because they’d thought a bomb might be inside the bags. Otherwise, they would have done it themselves.

Now, Foster called Neil on the phone to meet up with him. Neil received a message on the phone with directions. He had no choice but to follow them, as he had got stuck in a corner. Foster also asked if there had been money in Jadea’s car and about the money they’d got for selling for Foster’s car. Foster told Neil to bring all the money to him. Foster kept on reminding Neil that he was the boss in this and, for the greater good, they were to follow his instructions properly. The diamonds promised were real, although such a burden would sound like a lie at first.

Tinashe regretted his decisions, but what is done is done. Tinashe had agreed to participate in the robbery because of a few hundred but in the end it turned out great for him. He was not just a random choice from the crowd. Tinashe's drug abuse status had never been higher when Tanya showed him the rock of death. They would be like zombies – partying all the time, often with women. A lot of call girls and other girls would use drugs with them. Tanya was likely to be HIV positive, but he never got to the point of being tested for the virus. As a joke he said, "I'd rather not know about it than live with it in mind."

Tinashe could see how crystal meth was stealing his health away and for Tanya it was worse. Sometimes it was as if he were a corpse amongst his people, because he could be stiff for hours.

IT WAS AROUND 6PM WHEN George made his way to collect his parcel from the security bank. They do not care where the money comes from. Their job is only to keep it safe for the owner. He used an ordinary car with tinted windows. He was wearing a national rugby cap, red tartan shirt and black jeans.

George was not sure about leaving his things in safety boxes again. A report that had gone viral the previous year about such boxes being tampered with made him nervous. He'd read in a newspaper that there were about forty-six safety boxes that had gone missing the previous year. He knew such things happened and it made him aware of every kind of safety precaution that could link him back to his treasures. That evening he went to collect the bags and brought them safely into his care, much like God when He took His special possession out of slavery and carefully set them in the Promised Land. George wanted to show his son all the treasure that was to set them free forever from financial problems.

But meanwhile, the boys did a most foolish thing, being very motivated by the thought of being bad and true hustlers. They had bought some pantihose to hide their identity while robbing a liquor store. Tinashe went to spy and check on the tills. He only saw a skinny man as a guard, and he was not going to stop them any time soon because they could overpower him.

The jacket made Tinashe look muscular and he was scary looking. They came in running when the shop was about to close. They were screaming and shouting, "Everybody down, this is a robbery". They managed to get a lot of money and this was used to buy more liquor, more clothes, more shoes and phones, and to club hard. Looking in the mirror, they felt huge.

THE DETECTIVE'S WIFE WAS SCREAMING at him. She felt like he was hiding something. Cheating is not the only thing that breaks marriages, for other secrets can be as devious. She was not pleased at all because she saw that he was far away. His mind was still stuck with Zheng's words. Zheng had told him that he had a number of clients who checked out with the descriptions that Petrus had given him. This was accompanied by a copy of a video surveillance. This silenced him for the day and gave him heartburn. He might have got up to some less-than-honest behaviour in his work, just to pay the bills, but this left him dubious about the whole existence of the police force. Now he had witnessed another side to the man he had looked up to in honour, hoping one day to become like him. His boss had faded after he'd looked straight into the truth. Whoever gave him honour and a golden hand was as evil as he was. He thought about leaving all of this behind by resigning but thought that he had perhaps already signed up for his death.

Anna was getting impatient with Petrus' answers. George thought that sending him to Zheng was a peace offering and a bit of motivation. He'd misjudged by sending a tick to do the cattle's job. For Petrus, things were coming around; lights had started shining like stars near the moon. After a very long time of misery, he could see the light clearly. Compensation was going to work for him.

Whenever George approached one of these officers, he was about business and everything he gave them, loot or information, they needed. He did it because he wanted something in return. When he wanted to find someone quickly, he had spoken to the detective before Petrus. The detective wanted some money at some point, but when the offer from another individual was bigger, he'd turned against an old friend. He wanted to put George away because of a different influence. He worked for the highest bidder.

George had doubled up his security base, so that he would not get shopped in the process. He'd shown him more information, and explained about how bags with illegal stones were still being moved beyond the borders. They'd made a partnership through this and the detective had also tried to locate a woman George was looking for during that time. He had inadequate information about that woman's location and it was bad news for George and some people started noticing the dirty games that the detective was playing, and got angry, saying that he had betrayed justice.

The time came that his loyalty by words was not enough; he surely had to prove he was worthy of trust.

PETRUS HAD THOUGHT THINGS THROUGH and resignation was not going to solve any problems. His plan for the future was to send his children to university someday. Withdrawing from this case was not an option at all; it was opening some door of revelation to new power. Often, power comes with threats and to ensure the safety of your home is a good precaution.

JOEY CONSIDERED GEORGE'S ESCAPE. SOMEONE must have helped him out and the argument about whom remained controversial. His instincts were correct but proving it was not that easy and not even helpful. If it was a missed lead they would have blamed or pointed fingers, but in this instance it had happened in their own house.

A specialist had come in to look around and tell them what might have happened. After being pressurized, the policeman who George had injured tried to explain what had happened. When they checked later at the evidence that George had tampered with, only blank white sheets were found inside of the folder. Surprisingly, evidence that Petrus had stored in his office, including bullet fragments from the victim's body, were also missing. They came to the conclusion as a whole team that he had tricked them into arresting him, so that he could wipe out all the information about himself. They became more suspicious about the station, wondering if it had bugs around.

A SHORT DAY IT WAS, when young boys were turning up in one of the hottest clubs on a rooftop to drink expensive champagne and listen to music. It felt like Tinashe's ambitions were at last coming into being. This is what he'd always wanted for his entire life, so he took the chance to enjoy it. Age restrictions at club doors stopped him a few times, but the guards accepted money to let him in. They blew what they had, hoping to get more the next day and become even richer a day after that. Like brothers, they tossed to the new life, but Tanya urged: "Business comes first".

"Just think, with the new money we can have a mansion and big studios. In this way we can even start that fashion shop, you have always been talking about."

Chapter 13

Foster had an appointment with Choo that evening. His shoulder was in good shape. Foster's interest was in clearing his name as much as he could. At last, Foster found what he wanted from Choo and that was his word. He explained that whatever these boys were doing, too many people were getting involved and it was becoming very dangerous. The BMW that had been in front of the police station but the car had not been driven by Foster, and yet the car belonged to him. Stanley had only reported it missing after the situation had got worse.

When he got home, astoundingly, Joey Morish was sitting inside Foster's house on the couch, his gun laid on the table. "You are a very difficult man to find, Mr Stanley. Have you been doing business lately?" Joey asked.

"Why is this man in my house again," Foster thought. Foster walked in feeling disrespected, but he had no choice but to go along with this because he had signed up for it. He walked in and sat on the other side on the room, facing Joey. *"I should have killed you a long time ago,"* Foster thought to himself.

"I have been looking for your car. I tried the garage. I suppose a taxi brought you here?" Joey said.

"I just reported it missing. Did you check with the other police officers?" Foster replied.

"I hope you are not helping him again, after he tried to kill you! I saw it the very same time that George escaped. I bet he used your car as a getaway somehow," Joey developed this theory, while explaining to Foster, who was in the dark about all of this. "So I will ask again, did you help him escape? Maybe this time he offered you something besides a bullet."

Foster was astonished by this. "When and how did he escape? I thought you had all the big guns," Foster continued making a mockery. "I am not the only one who is having bad luck today. Did you see the man who had my car?" Foster asked.

"I saw an average height guy, dark in complexion. Does that sound familiar?"

Foster denied knowing anyone like that. He came up with his own theory. "I think they stole it from me and used it to distract you during the hour of escape." He then added, "I did not help that monkey in any way."

"I have two options for you: A and B. Option A: help us to kill this bastard; and Option B: that gun on the table will decide that for you." Joey made his statement clear.

"Ease up and relax. I got you bro, and this will be my pleasure anyway," Foster replied. "But if we work as professionals, I will not do this for nothing because my life is on the line here," Foster added.

Joey agreed to this deal for this was the only thing he had so far. They promised each other to deliver and only faith kept them going. They all wanted to play a vicious game but things were not working out for any of them.

JOEY'S WIFE LISA WAS ABDUCTED that same night. Joey was starting to work things out. Lisa was in their hands and he had to destroy George first. He was enraged by this news, and very afraid for his pregnant wife. They'd made a fool out of him. For more than an hour, he was discombobulated by the news. He thought it was some sort of a prank and he tried calling her, but the call was not going through. He wanted to fight for what was his.

George had screwed up and rumpled their lives. Getting one visit from George was as if it were from the devil himself because it left everyone broken apart. The scripted information on a flash drive was dangerous in the right hands. Money and diamonds did not matter at all from this point on. It was only a matter of time before Joey had lost Lisa forever. They changed agreements and forced Joey to operate differently: this time better organised.

TANYA WAS HAVING FUN WITH a random girl he'd come back with from the club. He had no idea who she was and figured he was not interested in getting to know her anyway. They both only wanted to have sex, nothing else. She came along with her friend. Neil was not around and Tinashe was playing games on a set. Tanya convinced the other girlfriend to have sex with Tinashe. They were all drunk and still smoking.

This marked Tinashe's first time and Tanya whispered to him that he should wear protection just in case. Everything happened straight away for these young 'ballers'. Tinashe wished this kind of living could last forever; all his problems had disappeared. He thought about the claims that George was his father. He didn't care; all he wanted was more money. He wanted more drugs and alcohol.

When Tanya melted crystal, Tinashe was there. When Neil was snorting cat, Tinashe again would join him. His was a corrupted young mind consumed by horror. This happens when parental guidance is insufficient or thwarted. Life gave him rules and then broke them, and that led him into this inconsistency. The best food he'd used to get was the leftovers from fast food restaurants. When he begged, the people he asked for money thought that he probably wanted drugs, and walked by. Tinashe could not read and write; he could barely hold a pen correctly. Whatever it was going to take, he vowed never to go back to that way of living.

When they had sat down to listen to music, Tinashe remembered the gun that Foster had thrown into the water. He told them about that and said how useful it could be in the near future. He kept on surprising them each time he opened his mouth. Leadership comes from a jeer. He looked at his neck and the chain that surrounded it; the wrist was ice cold. Looking back, all he'd every done was window shop.

FIFTH DAY

EARLY THAT MORNING, A POLICEWOMAN knocked on Petrus' home door. She asked the detective if she could take a look around the house and in his car too. She first told him, "We believe your car was used in a hit and run". She told him his car had been identified by a possible witness.

Unfortunately, a misinterpretation of information had happened. The car she had mentioned had been sold about a year before, after problems with it had kept him stressed. She asked to come in and this roused the detective's instincts. "*Something is probably wrong here*," he thought. He told her that the family was still asleep and he'd rather change first. That gave him the opportunity to wake his wife up. He told her to take the kids away using the back door. He told the woman that had worked for them for a long time, "Go and tell the policewoman to wait in the back or at the station". He ran to the car and drove his family away. The woman in the police uniform received the news. Real smooth, she did not argue, but left quietly.

Petrus, driving down the road, saw two cars that were travelling fast. He assumed these cars were heading to his house; he feared that danger. He also feared for the young man who was helping him with all this. One of the people who worked for him had already been apprehended and charged with identity fraud. They claimed he'd impersonated a forensic investigator. They'd arrested him to find out where Detective Mduduzi was. The truth that he wanted to expose was a scandal. It was left for him to decide either to continue with this or to run far away forever.

At some point he thought, *"The only way of getting this case buried is money"*. He'd played too close to the fire and it was starting to burn him. His wife looked at him angrily, but she was happy that the whole family was together. He told her, "All this will pass like the wind. I just need you to be strong for the family". Detective Mduduzi's thoughts were rattled as he did not know if his family was going to be safe at all. After driving for two kilometres, he got out of the car. He gave Anna some money and told her, "Take the children to my mother's house". She would do as he said, but she argued that he should go with them. He left her yelling, knowing she was going to be okay later on.

He looked around for a meter taxi, but did not find one. He stopped another driver with his badge and demanded she take him to where he was heading. She drove him back to his home and she drove very fast, fearing for her life. The detective got out near his house and walked. He gave the woman some money for the used fuel.

When he got to the house, the cars he'd seen while driving his family away had parked in front of the yard. His house was upside down; they were invading his privacy. The girl he had left inside the house had been threatened, so she sat quietly on a chair. Anything was possible from this point onwards. They told her that disrupting an investigation was a crime and, like all crimes, it had its consequences. She had zero knowledge of what was going on, and none about her rights as a human being. She took the instruction and sat down. She saw Petrus and jumped into his arms happily.

One of the guys walked up to him like he owned the house. They asked him for an explanation as if he owed them one. When they left, he did not object to going with them. Objection leaves a person falsely accused. A Dr Kong – his name was derived from the movie King Kong – asked him to come inside, so that they could avoid an unnecessary arrest. He did not question it further. They had certain charges against him, besides a poor hit and run allegation. Dr K decided to take him for a ride because he was in charge. It is strange for a police officer, especially a detective such as him, to be arrested without a forty-eight-hour warning or a warrant. Something was up and the dots were starting to link up. Making a deal with the devil just to prosper, turns you into a puppet with a lot of issues.

FOSTER SETTLED ON GOING TO see the boys. One had visited him the previous day. Foster needed the whereabouts of his stolen car. His shoulder was healing faster than expected. He took the description of the man that Joey had given him and started using it for his search. He knew one place that could give him answers, without him dragging around too much. Africano was a place where stolen cars were sold. He visited the Africano junk yard driving a borrowed car. The men at the yard were legit. Foster knew them personally because they once had done business. He slowed down as he approached. The weather was a bit colder than usual and the men surrounded a drum with fire that was burning tyres. They were smoking and cracking jokes. He joined them with a warm greeting. One of them searched him for a weapon; most of their business associates carried dangerous weapons with them.

They laughed together for a few minutes and then it was time for him to tell his story.

"Hello, Stanley," Aligi, the owner, recognised and greeted him. "I thought you were out of the business," he said.

"Look man, I'm just a visitor," Foster replied. Later on, Foster asked for a private conversation with Aligi. They both walked to Aligi's office, and Foster pulled out his phone to show him photos of his stolen car. He asked Aligi if in recent days he had not seen it around or heard about it. Unfortunately, the answer was a "No". He asked if maybe some of his guys might know about this. When they were leaving the office, showing the photos around, one of the boys said he had seen it but, disappointingly, he knew nothing more about it.

It was a forty-five minute drive from Africano to crossing the bridge into his usual road. His mind and heart could not think about anything besides money. He'd risked everything, including his own life. Some people would call him "notorious", and they knew exactly who he was.

He arrived at the place Neil had told him about. Neil played middleman between Tinashe and Foster, and Tanya remained the watchman all the time. This was their opportunity to rise from the ground and make it into the new money. They dreamed of living uptown in an expensive big house with a jacuzzi and a garage full of fast cars.

Such a life had become what this generation calls freedom. They wanted never to worry financially again. Economic freedom is what they scream for and dream about. The youth use drugs for relief and the promotion of drug use is viral.

Drugs are no longer the only problem into today's society. Technology is, in fact, so hyper-arousing that it raises dopamine levels, the feel-good neurotransmitter most involved in addiction, to the same extent as sex, drugs and gambling. Researchers have shown that digital devices and social media are addictive. Some researchers call it "electronic cocaine or digital heroin". Social media and screens affect the brain's frontal cortex in exactly the same way that cocaine does. These are essentially digital drugs.

Foster surprised the boys with his arrival. Tanya and Neil were still asleep but Tinashe was on the roof, staring at the city lights. When Foster knocked on the door, Neil was surprised into opening it "*How did this guy pass the security check downstairs*," he thought, but that did not matter. He greeted him with a smile. "I was not expecting you as early as this," Neil said when Foster walked in.

"Because of this weed you smoke, noon is your waking up time," said Foster walking into the house. "Tanya is still sleeping but where is the Dope?" Foster asked. The "Dope" he referred to was Tinashe.

"He borrowed my lighter and he is smoking, probably."

“Call him, and also wake Tanya up,” said Foster.

Neil went to one of the bedrooms to wake Tanya up, then to the roof.

There were two bottles of whiskey on the table. One was empty, the other was closed. Foster stood up and reached out for it. Next to it were glasses. He took the bottle and poured whiskey into four glasses.

Tanya was stretching his muscles and wearing his white vest. He was surprised but not shocked to see Foster. Just seeing him around felt like hardcore money was coming. He took his chain and walked towards Foster. Neil walked in and Tinashe followed behind him. Neil had only told him, “Someone is here to see you.”

Tinashe had got anxious. “*Who might this be,*” he thought. “*Maybe George has traced me using my phone call.*” He’d thrown down the cigarette and stamped on it with his new sneakers.

When he walked into the house hoping to see George, it was Foster “the baby keeper” he found. After the salutation, they gathered before Foster as he gave his speech. He gave them whiskey shots. “Ease up on that, young fella,” he warned Tinashe.

“Now,” he said, “everyone clasp onto your seats”. He exhaled for a moment. It seemed as if it was such a long journey type of conversation. Again, he exhaled and gulped in as much air as he could.

DETECTIVE MDUDUZI WAS STILL IN the car facing questions. They placed his life in a spotlight and truly cornered him. They asked a lot about him and the other officer impersonating an IPID officer. What was his concern in such a private investigation? Why would he do that anyway? This was the concern of a big black man who was sitting next to him. It was clear that he was in charge here, although taking orders on the phone.

Petrus kept on arguing with them. “I have no idea about these accusations and where they are being driven from but I am a true officer." They stormed him with bad news only. This whole interrogation was illegal in the eyes of the law and these men feared for their lives, so they only acted like this to read Petrus like a book. It was tough to knock him down just like that. He clearly saw how foolishly they were trying to toss him, like a coin. Many officials were involved in this mess and a few families were living nobly out of the proceeds. But the pressure gave Petrus motivation to pursue this to the end.

"What is a crime, Detective?" Dr K asked him. He was not sure how to answer such a question, but he replied, "An act punishable by law; usually considered an evil act. Some dictionaries refer to it as an evil act necessarily punishable by law."

Then he asked them, "Are you going to charge me with something because if not I really have to be somewhere else." They tried the simple ways but the detective was well informed. Eventually, they took him to another police station and charged him with fraud.

"You are not the right person for this job you have," Dr K said. "This is not just the end but also the beginning of your suffering. Make any calls you wish," K added.

The evidence he depended on was still in George's hands and there was a notebook that he kept to himself. He was never going to let it go easily. "This is my job!" he exclaimed.

After having the whiskey, Tinashe burned out and felt paranoid. He asked for a cigarette just to smoke again on the roof. They gave him one, but he ran downstairs instead of upstairs. They were worried because that seemed very suspicious, so they followed him. They knew after he'd gone out that something was way off in his eyes. One ran upstairs and two ran downstairs. Neil called out, "Wait for me, I need a smoke too."

Only the day before, Tinashe had been locked in a boot, kidnapped by Foster's cousin. Trusting people had become an issue. He was no longer looking for anybody's help. He ran down the stairs from the eighth floor. Foster quickly ran to the lift to wait for him on the ground floor. He hoped to catch him in time. This time he was no longer playing easy. He wanted to tell Tinashe that the kidnapping had nothing to do with him. A chameleon changes colours unexpectedly, just like a snitch.

Neil followed Tinashe, hoping to catch up with him. After he saw a flash of Neil on the third floor, Tinashe assumed someone was waiting for him downstairs, so he took another turn. He ran into the passage to reach stairs situated outside the building. They took him to the next building. His strategy worked and he escaped and walked down through the second building against the hotel. Neil could not find him anywhere and wondered how he'd lost him.

Neil and Foster looked at each other empty handed. They thought he might be out there in the streets or somewhere in the hotel hiding. The CCTV would be able to identify him in any corner; they talked to the security guards, claiming there might be an unauthorised person in the building.

Tinashe had no worries about cameras watching him. He used option B to survive while others were looking for him. He had enemies and a ton of snakes calling themselves friends. It took time until the full security check was finished.

Tinashe took the cigarette, a lighter and a phone that belonged to Neil. Becoming familiar with phones that did not belong to him was becoming a pattern. His heart pounded like crazy and goose bumps appeared as if the temperature was minus two degrees. He kept on looking back, like a woman who'd ditched a foetus in a bin and feels like someone is watching and following her. He was worried about his life more than ever.

Detective Mduduzi walked into the office of his Colonel charged up. He'd made calls to his people and they'd released him without any debate. His family was not safe as other officers had started neglecting him. His eagerness to find a way to get rid of the greedy bastards was making him unsteady.

When the Colonel saw his face burning so fiercely, he said, "Please take a seat". He begged him to avoid unnecessary dramatics because some dangerous people were listening. The Colonel knew how inundated Petrus had been and he wanted to find a solution for him. Petrus pulled out a chair and sat down quietly. "Can I ask something?" his boss asked.

"Yes, yes," the detective replied repeatedly. "What is it?" He was eager to hear whatever his superior was going to say. The Colonel however opened the table for a proper discussion.

Petrus cut him off out of anger. "Are you involved in any of this?"

The man learned back against his chair and he removed his reading specs. He avoided looking into Petrus' eyes a couple of times but he stood up for himself like a man confident enough to set Petrus straight. "No, Detective, and I have been protecting you all this time but now that you have decided to be a man, please go for it. Wrath is going to hurt you. What made you think I would be involved."

Petrus replied, "It is because my family's safety is threatened and it all happened after I talked to you about this. I guess you blew over to someone else."

"What do you mean, your family is involved now?" the man asked.

Petrus gave a short summary of what type of terror and horror Dr K had promised him. He made it as short as he could, although the Colonel kept on asking him about precise details and descriptions of these boys, because the name was very new.

"The lack of evidence will destroy my career," Petrus thought. George had swept that evidence under the carpet for his personal use and considered it as insurance for the days to come.

The Colonel said the case should be closed and investigated no more, for they were losing more than they were gaining. Lives were not worth losing, especially those of the innocent. They wanted to be at peace, with happy families, and not in a never-ending war.

TINASHE HID AND RAN FROM his syrup-stoned friends. He thought of running to Makhathini, but things had changed between them. Tinashe promised himself never to smoke that cream powder again. Nyaope is nothing but Lucifer himself. He started going in the direction where he could find his old friends. It was quite a distance to get there by foot. By the time he got there, an ambulance was carrying away a cold body after a drug overdose. This was not the first time such a thing had happened. In fact, maybe twice a month, an ambulance would come to take some young person away.

He looked around, thinking, "*Maybe they have hidden themselves, doing the same drug that another had overdosed on*". They were all entangle in a web that was impossible to escape while breathing. When they had a taste of it, it was a sweet rose, and for sure they all wanted to have it again. They could never have enough to satisfy the craving. In the past, they had separated ways to hustle a few bucks and then would have a get together party. This drug is abusive to the users. Neither food nor safety matter as much as the drug does.

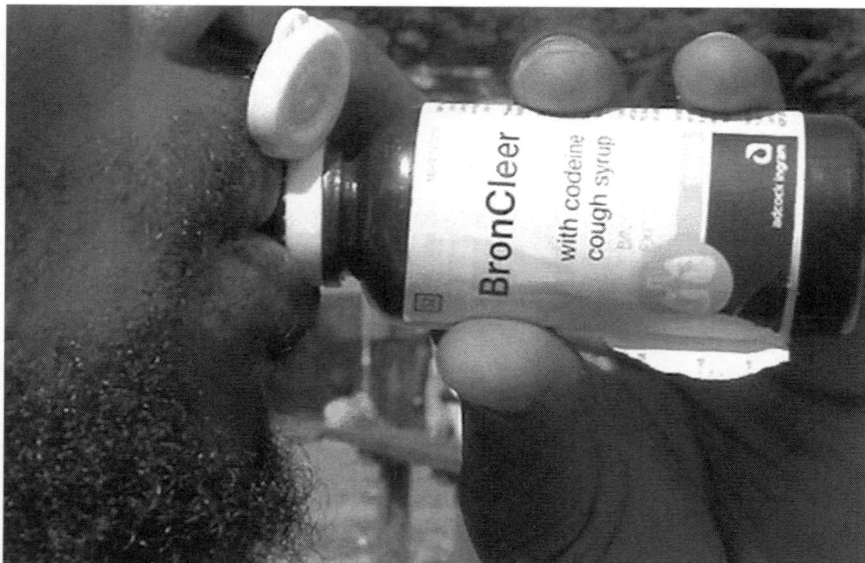

In the days with Tanya and Neil, cat and meth had become his new home, as well as all kinds of pharmacy syrups from purple to yellow. Suffering from paranoia was of the side effects. It made him think everyone wanted him dead. He was exaggerating about everything, somehow confused about everything.

MEANWHILE, DETECTIVE MDUDUZI HAD MADE a turn to Joey, hoping to hear about the boys' whereabouts. They seemed to have disappeared after they could not get hold of George. The Colonel had set up a squad ready to take command, but Detective Mduduzi wanted to rescue and hear the words of his young officer. He thought it probable that his young and trustworthy officer had been arrested not because he was impersonating an identity, but because he had found something worth looking into. Through his instincts, he assumed that the young officer had a good explanation for the whole situation. A statement had been released apologising on behalf of the state, that there were no charges due to a lack of evidence.

Their conversation started in the car. The young officer told Detective Mduduzi about how biased they were. "These shipments are made in southern Africa and people are getting more and more corrupt," he said.

Petrus the detective wanted specific names. "Why do they get paid such amounts while we are busy catching rats?"

"It is a game. Either you accept or you die but nobody ever took a chance to reject such fortunes. The money from the diamonds should be used for the development of infrastructure and the economy as a whole, but instead a few individual have gained a lot. Many illegal co-operations, organised crime groups and traffickers are doing well because of this," he replied.

"Many diamonds are exchanged in real markets but never shown in the books? Why is that? One misunderstanding can cause a whole lot of problems to everyone," the detective interfered, "and a good example is George's rebellion".

"Yes, Sir. This is the biggest organised hustle in the whole of Africa. Those with enough political power are eating from this, especially the Zimbabweans and Congolese, and other politicians have reached new heights out of it and yet the economy is crumbling and people are hungry." He added, "They are protecting each other; not each other as such but they are protecting their interests by killing those who raise a voice against them. We are looking at the biggest gang in Africa," he finished of.

After the detective had heard this much, it was clear to him that he was a simpleton. A preliminary investigation had led them to this. He knew that the boy was important and George could exchange information with him in the deal. If he was going to bring down the bosses, he had to be well equipped for that. Some of these people against whom they were about to open cases were paying bribes to other trusted individuals such as Joey to hide these allegations.

In addition, it was obvious they were going to cross paths at some point and the bull's eye was the target. They could not meet but a call made it possible to talk. "How come we are both stranded in a corner, trying to be free, while they play with us as if we are toys?" Joey Morish asked. Petrus walked into the room like seven wise wonders, as if he had it all figured out.

Mbali had explained a few things that did not make sense at all to Petrus. At least it was an eye opener for watchdogs out there. They jumped to work later on. Petrus asked if they knew the whereabouts of Jadea. His disappearance from the probe was suspicious but reasonable after the issue with Joey had happened. Joey's delegate explained that they had wanted to take the stolen items to the rightful owner in order to avoid outright war.

Foster decided to change the apartment he was living in, for safety reasons. Since Joey had made another visit the night before, he had felt anxious. A visit such as Joey's brings only trouble after two or three visits. When thinking about it properly, his personal space felt invaded. He no longer felt uncomfortable while trying to fall asleep on his bed. His thoughts kept on reminding him about his friend, who had been shot while asleep. He found another apartment and, while wary, he felt safe. Foster was working out plan C, since George had ruined plan A and Tinashe had run away.

Their search for Tinashe had lasted about any hour. Foster had told them to bring the car they had. "If you find him, call me. Do not talk to him but follow him." He told them the same thing over again, as they switched cars.

A couple of minutes later, his phone rang. Petrus wanted to talk to him. "Can we meet at my station?" Petrus asked. "There might be an issue up here." Foster told the Detective to expect him in about an hour. Petrus needed a troublemaker to cut down the long rope of corruption among company executives and government officials and, if necessary, to make an alliance with a small devil to take out a bigger one. The murder that had happened years ago had left him traumatized and with one objective, and that was killing these bastards.

AFTER ONE HOUR HAD PASSED Tinashe had traced Makhathini, who was sincerely sorry about what had happen before with Jadea. It had not been an act of betrayal, but of brotherly love. In his mind he was helping, but could not read the signs and between the lines. Tinashe tried to explain but his words were just bumping on walls. Whether he understood him or not, Tinashe decided to stay away from him.

All this time, Tanya and Neil were watching closely after they'd successfully traced him. They knew his exact moves within a short time. He might have told them what he would do if anything happened.

FOSTER WAS LOOKING FOR JADEA. It was going to be a wrath of a menace, a quick lighting of a dawn attack. Foster's heart and money were inseparable. Most educated people in the world are spending more time calculating ways to oppress the masses rather than finding ways to reach equality beyond social class. Foster's father had sent him to college growing up but the life he'd pursued had nothing to do with the degree. The streets had taught him how to survive, and ever since then street hustling had never stopped. At first he used to spend this money having fun, but later it was all only about the money.

After George had broken loose with his own files that also had Foster's name linked to them, he had more power over his opposition, but this power was not enough to grasp his son's love into the palms of his hands. He waited for Tinashe and it seemed like time was not moving at all.

In the same hour, Foster was at the station, trying to figure out the reason why they had summoned him. Another cop had walked him to the office and had left him outside the office. Their number had reduced as for their different reasons Joey and Jadea were not there.

"Here we go again, Stanley!' Petrus said. "These people are starting to come to my house, and I need to round up this thing within twenty-four hours before they extend their visits. I have one question for you: where is Tinashe? Jadea is also not here, and that makes me even more nervous."

Foster realised that his exemption from prosecution was still far away. It was hard for him to give up the young man advantage and, even if surrender meant freedom, he was willing to take his chances with it. The need to push him was there, but not in ignorant ways. He lied to Detective Mduduzi. "If I'd ever had him in my hands after Jadea lost him, George would have paid me off by now."

"This is no longer a joke, Stanley. Give me something to make it go away," the detective replied.

Foster's focus was only on himself and other people's lives did not matter. His lack of trust in the police made him hold back against them. "*When I am no longer useful, then what will happen to me*?" he thought.

"Use your ways to get to him because you once worked with him. You have been bragging about it," Petrus said.

Foster replied, "Talk to him as you did before," and stood up and walked out. He left Petrus burning out of anger and he worried about everyone knowing that he might have made some sort of a deal with George. His life was on a red light.

After Foster left, Detective Mduduzi called some of the officers he had gathered to follow Foster in a civilian car. They would follow him unnoticed once he started driving.

Foster drove away feeling boastful and comfortable and never noticed the car behind him. His thoughts were under pressure after what he had been through; he could not bear the pain of losing everything in one week. His time and faith both started fading away.

Chapter 14

Losing sight of the young boy was as painful as losing a lifetime opportunity. A life of lies and cheating destroys everything in the end. Foster made a plan, one of a kind, and he waited only for George to make a move.

Tinashe was obsessed with becoming a glamorous figure, getting rich or dying trying. He would see those who surrounded him using a syringe full of nyaope liquid mix. Tinashe had tried to talk them out of this, especially his best friend. He'd wanted to influence them to change their ways but they ended up influencing him most of the times. Drug abuse is slavery, not gangsterism. Nyaope users would rather share different viruses than stop using that drug. Use started as an experiment and addiction continuously grew. The end to some has come and some are still waiting. A few are making profits while many suffer.

Tinashe kept on looking at his phone, as if he were waiting for a call. Time was moving more slowly than anticipated. He could not wait to meet George because they still had unfinished business. The space for love in his heart was broken, but not beyond repair.

JOEY LEFT HIS BOYS RUNNING a macro computer system using a sketch drawing tracing the young boy. The liquor store robbery they had done was on camera. "Very close," one said and now strength of progress gave them motivation. It was not easy. Tinashe would change from "a" to "b" suddenly. His clothes kept on changing.

Everything was perfect outside for him, but Tinashe's eyes saw the security guard bleeding to death, and that kept on coming back to his conscience. This man had looked at him as if they had once met. He'd kept on staring at him and trying to avoid choking on his own blood. He realised that dreams and nightmares could live in the same room. Everything was no longer normal. "*The phenomenon of living a simple life is earned,*" he thought. Again, he realised losing life over material items is as painful as losing a soul in exchange for gaining the world. He saw it in that moment and swore never to turn back.

Seconds turned into minutes and minutes turned into hours, he was falling asleep, struggling to finish a cigarette. The phone he was using to contact George was safely in his inner pocket. And all the while, Foster barely slept while a dozen times during the night Tanya and Neil swapped shifts, watching Tinashe.

They cracked heads asking each other, "how long will it take to trace him from that store? As soon as George gets his hands on him, then we pack bags and leave on his victory."

Petrus did not want to hear any of this unbelievable bogus talk. They had snatched Joey's wife. They had done it against her will and used her as perfect bait. Their business was ruthless, and they could not afford a moral sense. How much Joey wanted them dead was beyond measure, but he feared losing his wife and all the wealth built through the years.

"Follow the boy and you will find your diamonds," Joey said while leaving the detective to do his work with the help of an unlimited external force. He then went to the rescue. Joey had enough equipment to start a war but he decided to negotiate and discuss his way out.

While on his way, Lisa tried to escape from her captors but that did not go well. She ended up with a bruised eye and then she started suffering cramps. Joey took out some of his own diamonds and replaced some of the ones George had stolen. That was what they had agreed to in order for them to release his wife.

Detective Mduduzi could not go home so he spent a sleepless night trying to figure out how to dismantle his enemies. Close to midnight, he phoned his wife, Anna. Hearing her voice telling him, "Everything shall be okay," was like a smile that thawed a frozen heart. She told him that the children had expected him to turn up, but they'd fallen asleep disappointed. Petrus was able to rest around midnight after chatting with Anna.

TINASHE HAD TWO DREAMS THAT each woke him during that night. The two dreams related in a superstitious way that he questioned.

He saw his mother approaching him from nowhere. Where she was coming from he had no idea, but there was a very bright light behind her. As she walked towards him, he recognised her and, surely, she was real in that moment. When he recognised her and walked towards her, she took his hand, held it tightly and started returning to the place she had been coming from. Tinashe felt his own heart pumping while he was in a deep sleep like never before. That woke him up and he did not understand any of this.

He did not wonder for long, trying to figure out the meaning of it. He took his cigarette and started smoking it. He only called it a "weird dream". He finished his cigarette and forced himself to sleep with one eye open. He could not afford to lose the phones he had, so he was checking them constantly. It was not as if the people he was with were not trustworthy, but taking such chances was a risk. The person who'd helped him with a blanket knew him well. They shared a trolley to collect plastic materials around the city. After reaching a certain amount of kilograms, collectors paid for it. On most occasions, the money bought food, cigarettes and weed.

He had another dream at around 03:00; it was different from the one that had woken him up earlier.

He dreamt of a greener pasture. He was getting into an aeroplane that had no specific destination. He felt the reality of it, as much as he fiendishly wanted it.

SIXTH DAY

EARLY THAT MORNING, POLICE SIRENS and ambulances were heard hurrying over to a murder scene. Neighbourhood residents digested a horror that left them traumatised. The homicide crew had covered the bodies waiting for a relative. They were asking questions about the incidents but nobody knew anything. The next of kin arrived and he looked very familiar.

Detective Mduduzi Mduduzi was falling to pieces. His whole family lay dead on the floor and he wondered, standing there, how he'd let it get to this. His eyes turned red from shedding so many tears. In that minute he was lost somewhere inside of him and forever gone. He stood around praying for a miracle, hoping it was a dream. His soul was lost and only a human vessel remained to deal with all the pain.

His Colonel heard the news and felt helpless while Detective Mduduzi could barely blink, looking at Thapiso's covered body. Corruption is a cancer protected by force and threats. Officers gathered around the detective to mourn with him. Those who had comforting words for such a time were saying them.

The good news that Joey's helping boys had all eyes on Tinashe did not matter anymore. Foster had led them to him. The damage was irreversible. That morning, the Colonel took over the investigation and his beef was with George. The detective went home, broken-hearted and ruined. He was trampled on like a rose. The reason neighbours had not heard any gunshots was that the killer had used a pillow to muffle them.

Petrus started mumbling through his tears, "I want my family back".

A newspaper ran a headline saying*: Policeman's family found butchered: three adults and two kids.* Rumour had it that the Basotho had played a crucial part in the massacre. They assumed that the detective had played them by letting George escape. Some of the money had belonged to them. They were lazy to dig but were hard workers when on a killing spree of miners, snatching the stones away with bullets. Those who suspected were sure about the Basotho's ugly record and that they had previously massacred fourteen people in a certain mining area. They'd confirmed Petrus' family details after they'd invaded his privacy. They traced frequent calls on his phone, so all they were waiting for was for him to make one last call. He'd signed his family's death papers when he'd decided to take down the impossible.

The Colonel went to the office just to leave everything in order and then left with the young officer to go to Petrus' house. He wanted to express the deep sorrow he felt about how things had turned out. They both came wearing full uniform as a sign of respect. The young officer rushed to open the door and let them in. Quietly, they walked into the house.

The Colonel had many words to say while in the car, but he became mute once he had stepped into the house. His thoughts could not find right words to express such a feeling of losing a family just like that. He tried his best to encourage. "Greatness comes from facing the difficulties of life. Sourness and rottenness turns into manure for a great plant to grow. Every obstacle strengthens the victim for the best or the worst." The Colonel looked at Petrus, hoping he would say one word just to express how he felt, but he remained quiet and they feared what he was thinking.

THAT SAME MORNING, TINASHE HAD George's number on the dialler. Knowledge is a skill and ignorance is a disaster designator. Tinashe called George that morning, at the same time that Neil had bought some juice and marijuana to drink and smoke in the car. They had long relied on fast food to keep them going. They did not want to lose sight of the boy and this way Foster wanted a counter attack on George.

While Tinashe was on the phone, many people were watching from hidden places. His doom was closer than expected and he was a subject of observation.

JOEY'S NIGHT WAS TOUGH AND very hard to get through. Joey had received the bad news and he was devastated about Petrus' family and worried about his own. His boys made progress as they were getting closer and closer to the mark but it was clear this all came at a very higher cost.

GEORGE'S AMBITIOUS MOTIVES TO BRING down the Basotho empire were completely out of the question. As it was, Zheng had mentioned that that empire was crumbling because of corruption and mass murder of innocent people.

However, the boy had come into his life unexpectedly and had caused a change of plan. Forward motion was on hold. George was afraid of losing it all. He was still guilty of murder and considered by some to be a suspect in Petrus' family's massacre. When he'd talked to Tinashe on that phone, they'd agreed to meet. George asked him to take a taxi and lose the phone.

TINASHE WAS WITH HIS FRIENDS, but he just left them without saying goodbye. He sold the phone to get transport money, and followed the instructions.

THE COLONEL KEPT ON CALMING Petrus down, but the depression was enormous. Petrus only said, "I want my wife and kids back." These were the only words he said all day. Those who knew him, could see how hurt he was. The murderer had taken away Petrus' wife, two children, a nanny and Petrus' mother. The killer had only left a three-year-old toddler. They were killed while sleeping, shot in the head while in bed and then leaking blood on the sheets. Maybe if the child were to remember something one day she would tell the whole story.

Family and workmates started gathering for the funeral. The evil had struck again and the house was ice cold. Petrus blamed himself very much because this was not an accident. He sought someone to tell him this was not real, even if it was a lie.

The morning investigation at the scene showed no signs of forced entry into the house. They started assuming that the killer was familiar with the house, or someone close to them had played a part. Nothing had been broken in the house, nothing worthy was missing and wallets with money were lying around. They were sure that this was personally done by a hired expert, and was not a robbery. The Basotho were suspected first because this investigation was going to drown them below the seas. "*They are still exposed to tribal wars*," an investigator mentioned to the reporters.

TINASHE HAD DONE EXACTLY WHAT George had said. It was around eleven in the morning when the young man walked into a five-star hotel for the first time. He reminisced about begging for food; he was only used to the bins full of leftovers. Since the time Tinashe arrived at the hotel, George constantly observed new unfamiliar movements.

"I am here to see George," he said to the female receptionist. Although he was wearing his new clothes, his night on the street had left him looking very dishevelled.

She thought, "*He is joking, right*?" She was judging the book by the cover.

"What is the room number?" she asked.

"Penthouse, 1309," he answered.

She dialled the number and instantly George picked up, "Let him come through, please. He is my guest."

She was left surprised, thinking, "*Is he for real?*"

She told him to take the lift. He was excited and nervous at the same time. He told himself, "I can do this".

Foster and some other goons followed all the way. They were taking chances and they worked out. Neil and Tanya had parked their car alongside a driveway. They exchanged vehicles with Foster, so they were driving a borrowed vehicle with circular designs all over it. On the opposite corner, few metres away from the hotel, a white local taxi was parked alongside an old building that had used to be a bank.

Tinashe's idea in visiting George had nothing to do with making up the lost time with his father. His motivation was currency-driven. To hate over a prolonged period will cause pain and suffering only to yourself. Hatred attracts negative energy that destroys everything in its path. There are no winners in this game.

The lift took him to the top floor and he stood facing the door. He opened the door and saw George's face clearly. George looked at him, ashamed that Tinashe had seen his worst colours.

"*This man is my father and I died twice in his heart. Never again,*" Tinashe thought. He looked at his father with an enemy's eye.

George hustled remorselessly. Now it was his chance to work things out. He had a lot of money, yet life had brought no joy to his door. After he'd heard about Detective Mduduzi's tragedy, he'd felt guilt that he was a catalyst to all of this. Money became worthless in that moment.

Tinashe stood waiting for business to begin and George had a speech set aside. He had laid the bags on the table. He said to Tinashe, "I am sorry for what happened in the past, but we can work things out from now on."

Tinashe took the gun he had stolen from Tanya. He pointed it at George. "I only came here for my money. I was not worth anything to you then and so why am I worth anything now?"

George was not shocked by the words but was surprised by the young man pulling out a gun on him. He wondered where it had came from.

"If money is what you came for, then here is a bag with money. Take it."

Tinashe moved to the bags and looked inside of one. The money in the bag was so much, far more than he had ever seen before. He resumed his position.

"Wait, before you take that bag outside," George said. "It is dangerous out there and many people are waiting for you downstairs. You can take the risk or you can stick it out with me. I will protect you here."

Tinashe replied, "I have been living out there all my life and I am the one holding the gun in this case, so you are likely to say anything to keep me under control."

"You are not listening. The detective who was investigating this case, right now he is mourning his whole family. They suspect me, but these men out there are ready to take you out for that bag," George warned, but Tinashe would not listen.

Tinashe took the bag and left. On his way to the lift, he placed his gun into the bag. He made sure no one was following him. He did not trust any of George's gimmicks as they sounded like fluff. Tinashe was excited. He got out of the lift holding his first time birthday package.

George walked over to the window and looked at his phone as it was ringing. Foster was calling. "*Why is he calling at such a time*? *This cannot be a coincidence*." He dropped the call before they even spoke. He picked up some binoculars and leaned against the wall, avoiding the balcony. Anyone with a clear shot would hardly spot him.

Tinashe walked outside and right away, as the door opened, he had a feeling that something bad was coming, but his bag gave him the insurance he needed most to ignore it all. He looked around and the place looked clear. Everything looked promising and real smooth, as planned, until a vehicle that belonged to Foster pulled over in front of him. Tinashe took two steps backs and stood waiting for Foster to get out of the car.

Someone else got out of the car. Tinashe continued walking. He thought, *"It was a false alarm"*. The man who got out, pulled out a knife and stabbed the young boy repeatedly. He took the bag and ran back to the car and drove away. The man looked suspicious as he wore a hood and leather pants. Those who were staring witnessed evil but could not help. Instead, they decided to take pictures. Someone driving that car caught Foster's attention and he followed him in pursuit. This caused great cries and confusion, and all the while Tinashe lay on the pavement, dying. All the cars followed the bag they had come for. It was a big operation when four cars pulled out of the hidden corners. None of them seemed to care about the young man.

George saw the BMW through his binoculars and ran to the lift. By the time he got to the ground floor, Tinashe was close to death. The knife had certainly done some damage. A receptionist who had served him looked scared from a distance and called the police. George risked his life by exposing himself when he ran to pick up the boy. He checked for a pulse first. A random car had stopped to watch. George took a jacket from one of the men at the scene and covered the boy. Quickly, they opened the car doors and got in carefully. He constantly checked the pulse and made sure that the boy was not choking on his blood. The driver had already located the closest hospital.

All the cars that were in pursuit attracted the attention of traffic police officers. These cars followed a fancy white vehicle that was increasing speed in the blink of an eye. Other vehicles that were following this car gave up quickly. Some of these cars could not keep up with the speed and they feared the angry police drivers.

When George got to the hospital, he left everything in the hands of the nurses and doctors. One of the nurses stopped George from going inside with them. He sat on the bench nervously, thinking about life. His thoughts started to run backwards over each piece of it. Tinashe's survival chances were slim. All he'd ever wanted was to cater for his family better than his father had done. In an effort to do so, he'd lost his chance to even have one, and he stood by himself. His shirt was full of blood stains. He asked himself, "*Where did I fail? Is it a necessity to own twenty houses without a family to live in even one of them?*"

Children have turned against their parents and blasphemers are the rulers of the world. Lawmakers are servants of the law, not masters of the law. A brother stands in front of the people and tells them exactly what they want to hear not what they have to know. Even when darkness falls upon them, he tells them, "*Do not run for your lives; everything is okay*".

We live according to a certain pattern that we cannot clearly see and we are in chains to it; it is slavery. We are urged to be competitive from childhood, one thing after another. This world will never build a society that brings the best out of each individual because free thinkers are condemned. Superiority is the greatest inferiority idea. No idea can ever be greater than God's and ignorance will destroy many fools. On the planet, we have enough resources to cater for everyone, but greed and selfishness are destroying it all. We live by default and not by choice.

George waited and waited. After two hours a doctor came back to him. "We have stabilised your son and it looks like we have saved him. If you had not been quick enough, it would have been something else. He has lost a lot of blood and we might need you to donate some blood for him." George replied and asked them if they could transfer Tinashe to another private facility. They did not argue but suggested it was not a good idea. Nonetheless, they wrapped everything up, preparing him for a transfer.

Another two hours passed and they transported him successfully. When they arrived, they took some of George's blood and tested it for any diseases but, unfortunately, the blood type was different from Tinashe's. The doctor told him to go home and rest. He kept on feeling guilty and wanted to surrender himself to the police. He'd made difficult choices in life and what he'd chosen had brought about unbearable consequences.

What he had in mind was to confess his whole life and to become a witness against all organised crimes. It was a good idea but he was never going to reach the courts to testify. He organised a very private and expensive room for Tinashe. Newspaper reporters felt left in the dark, they had no idea about the whole story. Police arrived later at the hospital, after they had spent hours trying to find it. George was in a position of having to choose whether to run away or face the worst. They wanted to bury him and he was worried, yet he wanted to see the boy back on his feet again. He had confidence that after all this nightmare better dreams were close.

He sat next to Tinashe, who had many machines around him and pipes running into his nose and mouth. He understood how difficult it is when you start caring for someone. *"If they were to arrest me,"* he thought, *"I will never come back again"*.

He also pressured the doctors to do the transfusion over night. Luckily, Doctor Choo decided to help him privately. Choo had helped George right from the beginning.

At George's request, they had also tested the blood for a DNA match. The tests and the results were not pleasant. As usual, the truth does have a habit of winning all battles and sets a heart free. Doctors cannot lie to a patient just to make them happy. The DNA did not match. Tinashe was not his son.

When he thought stress would be his own dubious playmate, bad news had eventually started raining into his ears. He had played his game well but not well enough. Another thing that had shown up was that George had cancer. This had gave him the chance to re-look his life. It had offered a new living that gave him more confusion about his choices.

He went and talked to Choo. "Tell me, Doctor." Choo only gave him a brown envelope. He sat in the office. Before opening the envelope, he asked Choo again for a favour. Choo replied, "Since I had you discharged from prison, I thought you were going to come along more often than the last time. Many people have come to me looking for answers for the past days. How much did you hit?"

George said, "Doctor, I am giving you the young man. He is of great courage and one day he will grow up to be a great man. You have raised your beautiful daughters very well and you are a better parent than I will ever be. Water and oil do not mix."

Choo spent much of his time doing research, evaluating scientific information and educating rural settlers about the best way of living better.

George added, "Leaving him in your hands might not be a bad thing because, once he goes back to these streets, they will kill him." George told Doctor Choo that, for now, "the wind is still harshly blowing against all walls".

After George had thought about it, he'd realised that his eager hunting down had caused such disastrous damage and caused such pain to different families. George stood up and looked at the doctor to warn him about old friends and phoney friends. When the knot of war is a tied rope, both sides ought to pull the rope from different sides with all strength. The knot will reach a point where cutting it is the only way to get rid of it. The focus is never to surrender, or rather never to start because quitting is hard.

WHEN THE BMW HAD TAKEN off, Foster had followed. Later, he thought of himself as a victim of George's foreplay. It was a checkmate. Tanya had experienced horror seeing his old friend being hurt, possibly beyond recovery. He'd thought he was hallucinating after taking some pills. The vehicle containing an unknown and dangerous individual had grabbed everybody's attention – and the money bag too.

Foster drove a Nissan GTI 16 valve. Neil and Tanya had exchanged it for the two stolen cars including one that had belonged to Foster. He figured it belonged to him. When Foster followed the car and passed a sign post, he thought he'd misread the sign. It took him two kilometres to realise the chessboard, and to realise that George was the target. As soon as this thought crossed his mind, he turned the car around without hesitation. He found police there and saw bloodstains along the pavement.

Foster looked around for something, but he only saw an old story in a book, He went into the hotel and asked a receptionist what had happened during the day. He was diddling around with his questions. He told her that he was going up to the room that the boy had visited. "It is a link to all this." He also mentioned to her that he was with the police private investigators.

Quickly, out of fear, she told Foster that the owner had already left.

JOEY MORISH WAS LOSING HIS mind. He dragged a chair over and brought it close to the bed. Lisa was in private care after she'd suffered a miscarriage. Neither could bear the news easily. This had been going to be their first child, and Joey was to name him after his beloved younger brother. He held her hand gently and he had more strength than she did. He avoided telling her what had happened to Petrus' family. Lisa had bruises below her right eye; it kept on reminding Joey that this was his fault. She repeatedly said, "My baby," countless times. Joey, as a man, wished revenge on these people because they had taken away his unborn child. Revenge was running down his veins as if it were blood and anger only spit in his face in tears; he could not hold them back. "*Laugh and the world laughs with you, weep and you weep alone.*"

Chapter 15

A month had passed since Petrus had lost his family. In the previous two weeks, Petrus had denounced his job and quit from the force. His health had deteriorated and his mind was a rough patch. Few people were still around, and most had gone back to their life problems.

Dr Choo's two daughters happily accepted Tinashe. The older was already married and the younger had recently graduated from a university. The doctor's pain in life was his wife, whom he'd lost to a road accident. The same accident had left him with metal in his kneecap. He'd managed to raise his two daughters as a single father and they'd grown up to respect him and love him. He'd felt proud when giving his daughter to her husband in marriage. It roused his best spirit and he'd wished his wife had been there to witness it. Unfortunately, death takes what is precious and leaves a mark of pain and hurt.

Tinashe was happy and healing well, although it had been a shock when he'd woken up in a room full of dolls and pink sheets that had once belonged to Choo's daughter.

It was the previous night that Doctor Choo had brought him home from the hospital. "This is your new home," he'd said. Tinashe looked out through the window and reminisced about the pain of street life: pushing trolleys, selling marijuana and begging for money and food. He felt that for as long as others were still out there, he would never be at peace until they were all free. Everything had changed though blood and pain. He looked at himself as bandages covered his wounds.

One evening, after he had lived there for some time, he got out of the bed and started moving around, going from door to door. Choo was home, and he heard the footsteps of the boy. His home had been lonely for some time because his girls had gone out on their own lives and only visited sometimes.

"Come and sit next to me," he shouted. They were used to each other now. Tinashe went to sit beside him, and took up a book from the table. "How are feeling today?" Choo asked Tinashe.

Tinashe replied in excitement, "Much better, Doc".

Doctor Choo had used some of his time to read interesting books to Tinashe and he had him hooked and eager to read. They opened the book and Tinashe led the reading as Doc followed him with corrections. Sometimes, to keep him motivated, he would say, "*Whoever loves corrections, loves knowledge but he who hates corrections is stupid*". After hearing this, all the embarrassment that he could not read would fade away.

Sometimes, he could not make sense of the words, but ambition to learn kept him going. They would relax and start going though letters until they made up a sentence. Sometimes they were on different pages mentally.

CORRUPTION IN THE POLICE FORCE caused many to be fired and the media revelled in the story as it escalated to the top ranks of government. But the heads were unharmed and business continued as usual, serious as it was. The details went viral: rumour after rumour and calamity after calamity. Everyone wanted to know the story and other conspiracies seemed real. Many individuals were brought in during the operation, both investigated and investigator. Still they did not came through.

A new female investigator in charge promised the Colonel she would unveil all skeletons. She was determined to get answers. She went to see the detective a few times and it did not go as well as she'd thought it would. Whenever she sat down with Petrus, she tried to ask about any leads as a head start, but every time she would go there, Petrus stood up and left.

Petrus was neither protecting her nor purely hating the force. The former detective was unable to distinguish between friends and enemies. He was a puzzle without pieces anymore. *"Am I ever going to happy,"* he asked himself as the pressure increased. If someone were to offer him death as food, he would not hesitate to eat and then ask for more.

TINASHE HAD SURVIVED DEATH AND things were not the same for him. Choo told him that once his body had recovered he would start attending school. Tinashe's face changed immediately. He was enjoying reading but the idea of school made him upset, but this conversation was not open for discussion. Apparently, he had no choice but to comply.

An enquiry was held into the officers who'd taken orders to hold Petrus in captivity. These orders never existed in any form in the system. The officer who'd gave them seemed to have disappeared. The entire operation was illegal. The officers were forced to return all the equipment that belonged to the government. They started looking deeply, either to cover it up or to get to the truth, but Petrus was not responding to any of it. He feared whoever they were would come back again to finish him off. He felt that he could not rest until the killer of his family was in a coffin.

Six weeks passed after he had lost his family. The Colonel came twice each week to check on him. He thought, "*Gaining the world and losing your soul*". Something clicked in his mind and he remembered that once a thief had said: "Crime is like a lizard tail which grows back after being cut off but if you leave it, it then grows bigger."

Two police officers guarding Petrus' house 24/7 were getting tired. They thought he was in danger, but especially from himself. During that week George came and sneaked into the house without the officers being aware. He'd parked his car in the next street. He found Petrus lying on his bed, face down. George opened the door and Petrus thought it was one of the officers checking up on him.

"What do you want now?" Mduduzi asked

"How are you doing?" replied George.

"Why are you here?" Mduduzi replied, reaching for his gun in a drawer. He pulled it out quickly.

"Oh! Wait, relax for a second!" The gun was pointing at George now. George slowly took out the gun he had and surrendered it to Petrus.

"How did you get in here?" Petrus looked devastated asking these questions.

George replied, "I sneaked inside. Petrus, we have to leave here or else they are going to leave you dead and the chances to take revenge for your family will be ruined. Most have been bankrupted and they are very angry."

"Who are you are talking about?"

"You will recognise their faces before death."

Petrus said, "I am not leaving with you, George. Thank you for the offer but I am in hell already, just waiting to die. They took away what I loved most, and if they even think about it I will drop them one by one."

All these words were bouncing back on a wall. "Good luck," George said. As he was about to leave, one of the officers was coming into the house, walking from the police car. The police car was at the front gate and George took his way using the back yard.

"Are you okay?" the officer asked, since Petrus stood staring out the window.

Petrus replied, "Do not mind me. Take a break and grab yourselves a half day."

"Are you going to be okay?" the officer asked again and Petrus nodded that he would be.

The officer walked out, surprised. This was the first conversation they'd actually had in weeks.

Hatred had consumed the ex-detective's being, and light had no space at all. He gave himself false hope as the pressure increased drastically. He held two guns in his hands that he'd retrieved from a toolbox.

In his hands, Tinashe held a glass of water and tablets. His body was recovering as well as anticipated. This was great news for him and the doctor. Drugs such as Nyaope take two weeks to get out of the blood system if the right antidote is used. The people who cook these drugs, they have an antidote for it but they never agreed to expose the recipe. They themselves usually take it and after two weeks they are healed completely from its effects.

Tinashe's thoughts would drive him mad from time to time, sometimes out of curiosity and sometimes out of drug craving. Choo had a private room in his house. One day Choo went to the hospital and Tinashe sneaked into the room. He was astound by the pictures that were in the room, especially one of a woman which was in a big frame. This woman was in her wedding dress. She looked very interesting, as if she were the Mona Lisa. This was Choo's late wife. Other pictures that surrounded it were those of family and friends.

Tinashe's interest in some of the art that was in the house grew. He walked around searching every corner of the house, hoping also to find money, or something he could turn into money.

After the officers had left, Petrus went into his sitting room and placed his shot gun on the table. He sat down facing his television as he started watching the news. For those thirty minutes, he saw his family as if it were a nightmare horror. An hour had passed since George had told him that leaving was the best option. He refused to be a slave to or the bait of corruption. He reduced the sound on the television, and he stood again, walking to the window. Two cars had parked outside, one black and one silver. He had goose bumps at that moment.

George saved Petrus. As the people in these cars were starting to load up at the gates, they received a call to withdraw from this mission. George had some information that was going to bury the whole mob. Quickly they drove off. People like these are ruled in blood and fear, and they had wanted to make an example out of him.

TINASHE LOOKED AT ALL THE art on the walls. Eventually, he picked up some white paper and a pencil. He tried to copy one by this artist who had passed by, selling his art to Choo for support. The house was full of pictures. The more he kept on practising, he more his drawings started looking as though a professional artist had done them.

PETRUS KEPT ON PAINTING THE picture clearer, building image after image. He had spilt innocent blood during his time of stardom. Innocent people were behind bars serving time for things they had not done. He had danced with the devil and it looked like it was going to last forever. He'd received money to cover up a crime more than once. He'd helped evil people to become more evil. He'd ignored the first warnings about his involvement in this situation and the consequences had been terrible. He'd taken the case because it looked familiar and money was in his best interest.

TINASHE LOOKED AT HIS ART closely. The angles on the paper were not the same as the ones that were on the original work.

That day, Choo left early from work and came back earlier than expected. He expected to see the young man watching television or playing games. He'd seen that Tinashe was getting more comfortable and had developed the feeling of being home. He had a new friend who would come and keep him company after school.

Choo went to check up on him in his room. They had converted the room into a boy's room. He was not there. "*Where is he*?" Choo thought, worried. He started thinking twice: "*Did he run away? But why would he do that*?" he asked himself. He was sure that running away was not an option for the boy, unless someone knew about him being there. A school had accepted Tinashe and he was to start the following term.

PETRUS SAW THE HISTORY OF his life in the blink of an eye. He'd caused pain to others and expected it never to come back to him. Those memories were a catalyst to increase the instability in his consciousness. His life was to change in an instant. He'd searched for peace but could not find any, and he'd searched for life but had found only death.

CHOO FINALLY FOUND TINASHE. HE had searched and got tired of it. He'd called his neighbour to check if they were playing there. He was about to call for a search party for the boy and he thought to himself, "*I have failed to keep him safe and secure*".

Whenever he felt pressured, he went to his room of memories to relieve his mind. Spending time looking at those pictures had a rather hypnotic effect on him. He blamed himself for the accident that had killed his wife. Even though years had passed after the accident had happened he still did not believe that God works in mysterious ways. When he opened the door, he found Tinashe and his drawings. These drawing unfroze a frosty heart because they brought a smile to Choo. He felt happy from within, although he had been angry just seconds before. One specific drawing silenced him, the one of his wedding day at the altar. He nearly cried looking at it. Tinashe's artistic talent was extraordinary and it had only taken him the copying of a few pictures to master how to hold a pencil well.

Choo took him and left all the drawings in that room. He told those that were helping him that he had found him. Choo's daughter had just arrived for the weekend, and she was amazed when she looked at the drawing that Tinashe had done. She was in one of the drawings.

Afterwards, they went out to grab a lunch together in a close-by restaurant. The weather was a little bit chilly so they grabbed their jackets. They suggested a movie, maybe after lunch.

Tinashe's first painting was later voted the best during a yearly exhibition. This was the beginning of something new.

As more weeks passed by, Petrus started going mad because of pressure in his mind. He hallucinated much as he started drinking excessively. Two prisoners in particular had been falsely accused and had lived behind walls for more than eight years. They had many rejected appeals. Petrus had played a part in setting up the evidence to bury these two people for a crime they did not commit.

The new female officer found a good start to investigate everything and understand why it had got to this point. "P*etrus was hiding something,*" she thought. Possibly, he also had connections to fraud, murder and all sorts of crimes that followed with it. He had power and pride. The female office knew she had stepped into the world of crime.

Petrus Mduduzi hanged himself in his bedroom: no letter, no nothing. What he had done in the past ate his soul, until he could see no option but to hang himself. An article later produced suggested that someone had killed him and had set it up to look like a suicide. The Colonel honoured him as a hero.

When George read about it in the newspaper, it did not come to him as a surprise. During the time he'd spent in jail, George had met a man in who was in his early fifties. This man was already serving his sixth year when George came in. A violent prisoner had once brutally kicked him in the head and had damaged his sight forever.

They became friends and one day he told George: “You cannot find lost treasure. Lost love is a burden to the heart and what we can find we have to treasure because you will never know how long you are Trying to remember the boy’s name going to have it. In the end, two wrongs do not make a right.”

Now George gave Foster one of his bags and wrote a note that said, “I forgive you.”